NINETY-SECOND STREET

BROOKLYN STORIES

BROOKLYN
WRITERS PRESS

GERRY COLEMAN

Published in the United States of America by the Brooklyn Writers Press, an imprint of Book Biz Hub, LLC

brooklynwriterspress.com

For permissions or information on bulk orders:
contact@bookbizhub.com

ISBNs:
978-1-952991-53-0 (e-Book)
978-1-952991-54-7 (Paperback)
978-1-952991-55-4 (Hardback)

Library of Congress No. 2025921421

First Edition

CONTENTS

ACKNOWLEDGEMENTS

Out of His League

Sarasota Scene Magazine 2020.

The Pavan: Arts & Lit Magazine of St. Peter's University 2022.

Winged Penny Review 2023.

Literally Stories: Short Fiction from Around The World 2024.

Featured Rerun, Literally Stories 2025.

The Story of Jimmy Gray

The Pavan 2023.

Literally Stories 2024.

Blood Lovers

Winner, Best in Short Story Category:

The 2023 Writers-In-Paradise

The Pavan 2024.

Literally Stories 2025.

Being Billy Olsen

Literally Stories 2024.

Purgatory Hill

Semi-finalist for American Literary Review's 2024.

Short Story Contest; Selected for The Short Story Workshop

at Writers In Paradise 2025.

Precambrian Hills and The Rock Coast of Brooklyn

The Pavan 2025.

Lil' Sistah

The Pavan 2025.

Snakes in The Garden

Literally Stories 2025.

Out of His League

"Love is a zero sum game."
—Billy Olsen

The Parrot Lounge
Ninety-Second Street
Bay Ridge, Brooklyn, NY
[Winter, 1972]

When Billy saw her, he behaved oddly, like a Cubist painting tumbling down a staircase. It was Tuesday evening. The Parrot Lounge's sole décor statement was a stuffed green parrot in a cage hanging from the ceiling below a light bulb, surrounded by cigarette smoke. Weekday nights were about nothing—talk, listen to music, leave early, get up for school or a boring office job. It was not the place to take a date or find a snug corner to brood in—too much light, too loud, substandard bar food, and flat pitchers of beer.

The Parrot stuck to the working-class, backstreet tradition for sideways-mobile singles and the struggling college crowd. People hung out with friends; some pushed tables together.

Sixties folksy pop music was on the jukebox: Simon and Garfunkel, Dylan, Jefferson Airplane, The Doors. It was a place to waste a few hours and punch in another day toward the weekend.

The neighborhood was not the best. On the washed-out periphery of New York City, the commute into Manhattan was an hour, and you couldn't see the Statue of Liberty even if you knew where to look. The neighborhood was also losing a bout of phony gentrification to pseudo-sophisticated eateries and half-ass woody pubs with cheap gas fireplaces named after romantic, mystical things: The Salmon of Knowledge, The Silver Apples of the Moon, and Where the Water Lilies Grow.

Billy Olsen looked at her through a three-ringed pretzel as she sat with her girlfriends. He had been looking at her for weeks. She was pretty and on the quiet side. She wore a red bandito-looking serape fringed with tassels that she fiddled with. Her chestnut-brown eyes were highlighted by coral shadows of teal and cobalt blue under black penciled eyebrows. She was perfect—maybe a little too.

He considered the salt crystals on the pretzel. Janis Joplin was complaining about something in the background—Awah, Awah, Awah, Awah—while his friends discussed how the Mets sucked. Each salt crystal was a tiny, white, marbled geometric fragment that glowed dully from inside when angled in the artificial light. He wondered how it was done—getting the salt on the pretzel distributed evenly across the circumference of the rings. It was as though little workers attached each crystal separately: intertwined, salted infinity loops tied in a bow.

Billy went incognito against the side window to cover a better view of the girl. He placed his glass on the sill and turned red next to the Rheingold Extra Dry sign. After staring at her long enough to get caught, he went to the bar for another pitcher. His friends, Eddie and Richie, presented their glasses like nestlings when he returned.

Billy Olsen conceded the Mets were not good. Janis absorbed his bluesy mood whenever he played her on the jukebox, so he fed it coins to match the girl.

She and her friends came every Tuesday night and always sat in the same chairs at the same table. She always listened patiently, attendant to her girlfriends—her smile fixed during humorous stories or frowning thoughtfully throughout if sad.

When she spoke, her comments were introduced by disclaimers and facial modifiers she tilted into.

"I don't know, perhaps . . . ," she'd say, or "I guess, I think . . . ."

She seemed out of place. Billy found that sweet. Perhaps she was out of place. Sometimes she would rustle for a moment, then reconnect with her friends. She had an extra pair of incisors on her top row that picked up smudges of bright red, purple, or pink lipstick. But the quality that leaped out, way beyond interpretation, was that she was in a fashion universe of her own.

The Parrot was filled with people in jeans and T-shirts or sweaters, while she tried out a Tang Dynasty–retro dress with flowing dragon sleeves for the first cool Tuesday night of autumn. One week she wore a Roaring Twenties flapper dress with a long stole around and down her shoulders and arms, with a rakish, tilted Gatsby hat on her head. The next she arrived in a bright, curtain-like Indian sari, diaphanous like see-through clouds.

She was out of his league. It was important to be in his league. But girls a little too this or too that were in his plans, because he was a little too himself. Shoot too high, and he was looking for trouble down the road. Go low, he already lost. Since his teenage years, he was more comfortable when his dates were more comfortable—in the same league. He had dates with girls who had acne, for example, who applied foundation shades that would not necessarily match their natural facial coloration or texture.

By the time they were back at the girl's door, her face would be cracked like desert sands. But suppose, just before he kissed her, the girl nudged forward a little teddy bear tongue from between her lips, ever so slightly. What pimples? Suppose she lifted her shoulders and tilted her face to await Billy's first embrace. He was glad to accommodate the inconvenience of the blemishes and the flaking makeup if the girl was that nice.

Being in his league was a series of compromises and offsetting compensations, but he was hardly perfect. The girls on the receiving end were prone to do the same assets-to-liabilities assessment. His hair was thinning at twenty-one. He frequently suffered cognitive fogginess when anxious and occasional childishly impish mood swings.

One Tuesday night endured a steady snow amidst the depths of winter, while Richie explained how his army reserve meeting went, and Billy Olsen took a flat beer to his spot by the bar's only window. The sill was a death destination for leafy, formerly flying insects to pile up for the Parrot's weekly cleanup.

He made a porthole with the heel of his palm in the condensation and squinted through the aperture into the unnatural neon glow. He looked through a life-sized reflection of his eye, which appeared outside in the storm, and imagined pigeons puffed along the cliff ledges of the apartments above the avenue.

Billy checked the girl out through a pretzel ring to see what she was wearing, when she appeared in the middle of a loop looking back. He made "Hi" with his lips. She made "Hi" back. He smiled. She looked away. When he least expected it, he was in front of her. She was alone at her table. Perhaps that was why he got up.

"Hi. Sorry for snooping on you through the pretzel. Your outfit is very nice. What is it, a poncho?"

"I guess it's a poncho. Or a wrap, perhaps."

"Sorry." He offered her his hand.

"I'm Billy Olsen."

Her left hand offered from under her wrap.

"Hello, Billy Olsen."

She was Gabriella.

They talked about ponchos and wraps and sun colors—things Billy knew nothing about. When her girlfriends came back, he returned to his table. Before he left for the night, he looked for her through a pretzel to say ' Bye," but she was gone.

The next Tuesday, taking the great-circle route to the bar with conspicuous nonchalance around her table, he said, "Hey, Gabriella. Nice cape, I think?"

"A cape. Maybe a blanket."

"I believe it's a cape."

"Could be."

It was a blanket, Lakota Sioux in design—a star quilt with bright reds, yellows, and oranges, clipped with a self-crafted clasp to hold it together with her head in the middle.

Taking Billy's lead, the guys, without being asked, carried their chairs to encamp at the girls' table in a coordinated, peaceful occupation. They had girlfriends, but it was not that kind of move. The Parrot was not that kind of place. The Parrot wasn't particularly any kind of place. Random conversation sparked around the table. People knew other people who knew someone else. This and that. Billy kept an eye on Gabriella, even though she was out of his league, even though he didn't expect a promotion any time soon.

Richie lit a joint. Teddy and Sal were behind the bar. They were cool. Richie was cool. He took a toke and backhanded it, waist-high, under the table to the girl on his left. The joint passed, cupped by giver to receiver to preserve the spark around the table. It was accepted to gift to the next. Some declined—no offense—passing it on by the wettened tip. Others made it glow red in the grottoes of their palms. Peace be with you.

When it came to Billy, he took a draw, hoping not to fall into a coughing fit, which he did. Gabriella's left hand came from under her Lakota blanket to rescue it into a lingering pull past her brilliant red lips and extra teeth into her lungs, which she held.

Richie drove some of them home in his father's 1960 Studebaker Lark. Billy Olsen and Gabriella piled into the backseat with a girlfriend in between. He tried to make eye contact, but Gabriella was happy to be the center of his attention from a safe distance.

John Lennon and the Plastic Ono Band joined them, jacked loud by Richie, who swayed with the wheel, and they all sang and swayed like the moon, the sun, and the stars along Third Avenue onto Ninety-Seventh Street and down Marine Boulevard.

Brownstones and row houses with stone stairs like miniature inner-city Aztec temples stood shoulder to shoulder on side streets to share laughter, nightmares, radio shows, and screams of love and anger through the walls. Constructed of sandstone extruded from condensed rock 250 million years old, the houses themselves were built only a hundred years earlier.

Billy Olsen tried to close in on Gabriella around the immensity of her girlfriend's overcoat, who continued to sway on and on, on and on with John and Yoko. He worked close enough to bombard Gabriella with battalions of photons shooting from his eyes, which he was unaware did not work that way—but so it felt to him, and so it felt to her. His eyes were a bland gray, like the Brooklyn night sky among the clouds above the streetlights.

The girlfriend's coat parted enough to allow him to touch Gabriella's shoulder with his forearm.

Billy Olsen was closer to her girlfriend's head than to Gabriella when he said, "Tell me a story about you."

He had waited way too long to ask her something meaningful.

"Please. You could make it up, and I promise to believe you."

"I don't have a story. At least I can't think of one." It was like her to say that.

"I can't think of a story about me neither."

Which was a lie. So he told her how he went to Newark to visit Stephen Crane's grave. His arm was now on the back of the seat over her shoulder. He told her how rain had whipped into his face. How he knew Crane's poems.

They were short, and there weren't many, so he recited what he could remember while standing over what was left of Crane underground. One about a man who ate his heart because it was his heart. Another about another ready to leap to his death:

"If thou and thy white arms were there / And the fall to doom a long way."

Billy Olsen didn't realize how nineteenth-century proper and corny this sounded to her.

"Just me and Crane," he said.

"The rain turned to snow, crusting my head and shoulders and Crane's grave white."

Also a lie. Her drawn eye line, bleak and perfectly curved, pushed into her forehead as she sat silently. Her eyelashes fluttered, reflected in the car window as Brooklyn flew by—lashes designed to slice a young man's heart.

They drove between cauldrons of sewer gas at the intersection near where the girls lived. Richie pulled up in front of their apartment building, turned to the backseat, his arm incidentally dropping over the girl next to him. "Here we are. Out you go."

Out they were.

Billy, with a long hike home in the storm, had a brief chat with Gabriella while her girlfriend fled in her overcoat into their building.

"Maybe see you next week?" he asked.

Her hair was parted perfectly down the middle and combed to slide alternatively from one side of her face to reveal the other if she tilted, which she did a lot.

He separated both sides with his hands to find her. Billy got the impression she wanted him to come upstairs. When they were alone in the elevator, they no longer thought about what either meant or wanted.

The apartment door was ajar on her floor. "California Dreamin'" drifted from her girlfriend's room. Gabriella and Billy Olsen sat on the sofa. She unfastened the clasp of her Lakota blanket to reveal an embroidered, carnelian-red percale blouse. Her right arm was willowy and handless, like the bud of an unblossomed flower. Gabriella touched Billy's cheek.

Something by Jefferson Airplane drifted into the room from down the hall. They listened quietly. He parted the hair from her face again to find her still there.

The Collected Works and Eternal Past of Johnny Healy

古池や
蛙飛び込む
水の音

—Matsuo Bashō, "Old Pond" Haiku
(17th Century, Edo, Japan)

The old men at the bar looked at themselves in the mirror fronted by bottles of whiskey everyone drank—mostly cheap rye, vodka, and gin—and oddly colored aperitifs nobody drank.

Old men's bars have mirrors for men to look at themselves looking at themselves. They gestured, blew regrets in cigarette smoke, some breathing it back through their nostrils and out again for a second rasp through the soft tissues. It was as though the three of us didn't exist, the way two species of birds might ignore each other out on a limb.

Our table was off the back room, lit dimly by the ambient light from the bar. It was furnished with a miniature pool table next to bent cues of varying thicknesses in a rack (no balls), a circular table for two (no chairs), and a dartboard on the wall (no darts). It was there to add senseless existence to the drab gin-mill aesthetic.

A tiger-striped cat, gray on gray with a square head, sat in a corner licking itself. It had no name. It made a cat noise when it saw me looking at it.

Eddie Costa, Kevin Dolan, and I sat in Mulcahy's Bar on the corner of Ninety-Second Street and Fifth Avenue with a pitcher of beer, waiting for Johnny Healy, who was late. We met in Mulcahy's every Thursday night since we were seventeen.

Eddie just wanted to know, "Okay, Dennis. What did Johnny do he needs to talk to us? Ride a donkey into class?"

Unlikely as that was, it was a possibility.

· · ·

Two blocks north was Third Avenue, which held a Guinness World Record for bars on one street and ran along the top of the terminal moraine, where the forward edge of the Laurentide Ice Sheet of the last great ice age halted, a mile high, to dump glacial till, sluiced sediments, boulders, and everything else it carried across the continent eighteen thousand years earlier.

It formed a highlands, or moraine ridge, for the avenue to run on top of for fifty blocks along Bay Ridge. Perfect for bars, for some reason. We preferred the funereal atmosphere of Mulcahy's down the hill, where you had to try the doorknob to tell if it was open.

"He'll be walking in any minute. It's complicated," I said.

Johnny and I were second-year English teachers at Hamilton High—a credible alternative to the horrors of Vietnam. Eddie, exempt from the draft, worked part-time in a deli. He had cerebral palsy after a trying sail down the birth canal twenty-two years earlier.

Johnny's brother-in-law, Kevin, taught gym at an all-boys high school. He smelled like a petunia after a locker room wash-up and was so convivial he would surely become principal somewhere within the next ten years.

Johnny Healy was less than a serious educator due to the excessive attention he devoted to his literary career, which had yet to emerge.

He created poems and stories in styles and shapes in fashion in his mind—then cut, puffed, or pasted them together for the right balance, for the correct emotional valences to strike true; for anyone to publish any part of it in any way, place, or form. Something they had failed so far to do.

Johnny stopped behaving like a normal person by the time we graduated high school. Along with his unfulfilled dream of being published, there was a tendency for personal mannerisms to take unpredictable, faddish turns.

If autumn was consumed by Ferlinghetti and the Beats, winter could find him as self-destructive as Byron or as sensuous as Whitman, as if he were discovering himself as he went. Without even trying, just to keep him in sight, I kept an extremely loose approximation of his false starts and cockeyed attempts at life I called my Johnny Story. Both his genius failures and unintelligible successes, whether intended or exploratory, were fair game for my collection. Boswell and Johnson. Guildenstern and Rosencrantz. Whatever. Better him than me.

After his marriage, he became increasingly Gallic, grew a goatee, and read Baudelaire in bed while Mary Ellen fell asleep watching him turn the pages. I worried he would get ambushed by life, like a moth playing Icarus with a light bulb. But his defining characteristic was a baffling literary tic.

The previous week, he gave me a haiku he had written that ran in my head like a playful earworm. It was beautiful. A child dives into a mysterious pond, triggering the sun's reflection to fracture into a million billion wavy pieces. He called it his "Pond Haiku." He discovered it had been plagiarized three centuries earlier by Matsuo Bashō, Japan's most famous poet.

Johnny believed legendary dead writers were retrospectively channeling his best ideas. Not all of Johnny's stories and poems were plagiarized—only the good ones. This made perfect sense in the personal way he saw the world. Bashō's pond haiku was not seriously similar, but it was seriously famous: same pond; a frog jumps in, not a girl; then there is a splash.

Johnny's version was better, but it wasn't Bashō. It was now worthless, perhaps criminal. I put the pre-plagiarized haiku out of my mind and into my Johnny file, which was growing more robust—but it continued to haunt Johnny to the degree he told his wife, Mary Ellen, who begged for the intervention of his friends.

Snow devils spoiled up and down the streets and alleyways. The perfect night to tie one on. A cloud lid had hung overhead for days like a beaten tin ceiling: no stars, no snow, no wind—as if the earth's surface was preparing for the Great Blizzard of 1971, which hit Brooklyn early afternoon Thursday.

I bought a second pitcher from Mr. Mulcahy. Still no Healy. The old fellas hogged the coat hooks, three deep on top of each other. We piled our jackets on Eddie's wheelchair, which we used to dogsled him down the block when it snowed. He was an octopus to walk home after a few beers.

Kevin asked, "Okay, Dennis. It's friggin' snowing; he ain't coming. So, what's with Johnny?"

"It's your sister. Mary Ellen's not happy with Johnny moping around. About a story this time. He told me himself—poems, whole stories—get swooped up in ass-backward ways. Remember 'The Girl Who Came Back'? About a girl who recovers from a coma?"

Eddie squinted at me over his beer.

"He swears it's been plagiarized. By a British dude been dead thirty years. Impossible? This is Johnny Healy we're talking about."

I took a flat beer to the front window in hopes of Johnny. I held the blinds back with my head to imagine pigeons puffed, unobserved, along the cliff ledges of the apartments above the avenue as snow curled around their hidden crevices.

I was perhaps beginning to enjoy myself. The headlights of a black sedan driving slowly down the middle of the street made the snow whiter, fall thicker—more severely angled in front of it. Its icy windshield wipers thumped to the ghost-wagon jangle of snow chains long after the car disappeared into the storm.

Back at the bar, jazz-era tunes played to aid the men's considerations after cycles of rye and beer. The whiskey opened sorrowful passageways to enter their bodies.

They sipped the level whiskey carefully off the glistening tops of their shot glasses—testing not to spill any until the glass could safely tip—then poured the rest in a slow, steady motion into their bodies, where it burned smoothly, at half-hourly intervals, to be able to say "good night" at 11:30 p.m.—as was the custom—and walk away home solid men.

"Shut—the—God—damned—door!" someone barked as snow and wind preceded Johnny into the barroom.

My head scrubbed the blinds like a musical washboard as he shut the door, did a clog dance, took off his jacket, and apologized for the rumpus.

We headed to our table. He took off a slush-crusted black beret with a little nipple on top after Kevin swiped at it. Johnny dropped onto a chair.

"What's that? Your mother's hat?" Eddie said.

Johnny was disinclined toward small talk.

"It's happened again. Denny'll tell you. I work for months on a story to find somebody's stolen it. Okay, stolen might be the wrong word, but I can't write for fear somebody's recorded it for previous use."

Eddie's head adjusted several times on his neck. Kevin jumped in.

"Johnny. Look. We'll have a shot with you. This will be good. You need psychiatric evaluation from your friends who love you. I don't mean to be rude, but there's probably ectoplasm displacement involved. We'll ask around. I'm buyin'."

"Fine. Look, shitheads," Johnny said.

"I told you guys this story months ago. A girl comes to, speaking a language nobody ever heard—from the earliest phases of humanoid existence, with memories of strange gods and frigged-up customs. They lay around humping each other in caves in the smoke from their fires, checking out the murky shadows they're making on the walls. And she's naturally scared to death of her modern friends and relatives around her bed, as they are of her.

"Her boyfriend shows up with a bouquet of flowers with ribbons around them for his Pleistocene sweetheart. Men fiddle with fedoras and ladies smoke cigarettes, wear high heels, their eyes mascaraed, and mouths smeared with lipstick. Like waking up after twenty centuries to find Lucille Ball waiting for you. Imagine?"

"Well, I still don't remember," Eddie said.

"It's been plagiarized is what matters. Found a story last month in an anthology written in 1939 by a sci-fi writer, L. Sprague de Camp, 'The Gnarly Man.' Same mashup of worlds: a woman falls for a Neanderthal in a freak show whose aging froze. It's eerie similar. Ape Man meets Homo sapiens, only the sexes are reversed. Mine is better, but what am I going to do? Who'd publish it?"

Kevin poured salt into the pitcher to give the impression of carbonation.

"So, which one was plagiarized? I don't get it."

"Neither do I, to be honest," Johnny said. "But it wasn't me."

Puddles formed under our table, including newly melted snow from Johnny's plastic snow boots.

The floor was 1920s black-and-white tiles, streaky from Wednesday's mop-down. Each tile was one inch by one inch and was diamond- or square-shaped, depending on how you came at them. Each was neatly framed by a thin, dark gray, almost black mixture of bucket juice, dirt, beer, vomit, and the dead and live microorganisms that held them fast like the grout they ate over the past fifty years.

Our heads swiveled again to the door moments after what appeared to be a Neolithic Iceman stumbled into Mulcahy's wearing blankets, rugs, and tar paper lashed to him like a winterized Brooklyn fig tree. As the room held its breath, he shuffled past the men at the bar in what looked like five pairs of pants.

"Oh, for frig sakes. It's Hickey," someone complained.

The name Hickey brought knee-jerk disgust from Benson-hurst to Red Hook. Children shunned him. Hickey was an urban legend along with the alligators in the sewers, where perhaps he lived himself. He did not beg and did not drink any more than most. An aristocrat among tramps, arrogant and disdainful, he did not speak unless he wanted to. His age was indeterminable; perhaps he wasn't real. Every Brooklyn generation claimed its own *Hickey*.

Hickey shuffled over to Mr. Mulcahy.

"Hey, Mr. Magoo."

Everyone gave him stink-space at the bar. It was impossible for him to wash in winter. He used gas station hoses in the summer. He would stand under an open nozzle fully dressed—a combination of laundry and shower—then he would dry off in the sun on a park bench like a sea lion on a rock.

He pointed to the overflow drain under the beer taps that dripped down a plastic tube into a white bucket.

"Any bar bilge?"

"You want this sewer puke? Yer not gettin' a glass and if yer not buying, ya can go clatter yourself, yer not stayin'."

Hickey pulled out a nickel.

"Here's the price of your bar piss before you flush it away for nothing."

"You'll have it for nothin'—then yer gone."

Hickey dug out an empty milk bottle among waddings of leaves and newspapers inside his junkyard overcoat.

Mr. Mulcahy took it to the drain bucket, poured what was there—flat and warm, including cigarette ashes and bug whatnots—into the bottle, which Hickey accepted with great tenderness, like receiving a basket of kittens.

"So kind of you. You shouldn't have. You didn't get any on the nice white apron, did you?"

Hickey clutched his heart and flipped the nickel onto the bar.

"Fair price. Sorry I'm not up for drinking with yourselves on such a lovely night. Ta-ta, ladies."

He nodded to the men at the bar like a Thanksgiving Day Parade balloon tipping forward in his giant snow suit.

"Oh, Magoo. Here's a shiny brown for your trouble." He pressed a penny onto the bar. Mr. Mulcahy lunged at a jar of pickled eggs to brain the retreating Hickey, meanwhile scattering miniature red plastic spears and lemon slices over the paying customers. The jar he could easily have launched onto Hickey's skull—if not for his barman's air, the object's dead weight, odd shape, and the shifting pink contents sloshing inside. He hugged the container to his chest as Hickey waddled to the door.

Before returning into the storm, Hickey turned to Mr. Mulcahy, rose on his toes over the men at the bar.

"Man, proud man," he proclaimed, "dressed in a little brief authority, like an angry ape, play such fantastic tricks before high heaven as make the angels weep."

Johnny's expression brightened. He guaranteed flat out he would write a magical folk story based on Hickey's life—a crib-proof, epic bio-poem in the Mycenaean manner, or after Kerouac in The Dharma Bums.

Hickey, Tramp Errant of the surrounding neighborhoods, had fascinated Johnny since childhood the way the dark both draws and repels the innocent. Hickey supposedly read Ovid's Metamorphoses to the animals while strolling through Prospect Park Zoo. Once, he shat on the mayor's desk in City Hall. Supposedly. Hopefully. Before he returned into the blizzard with his bottle of bar bilge, Johnny did the unthinkable.

"Mr. Hickey!"

Hickey stopped, his hand on the doorknob. The men at the bar turned to Johnny in disbelief.

"Will you have one with us before you go?"

Hickey said something in Latin. It did not sound like a compliment. Nevertheless, he made for our table like he had nothing better to do.

We accommodated to Hickey's presence by breathing through our mouths. I poured him a beer he took without acknowledgment. There was not the minutest thing to discuss. After an uncomfortable pause, Johnny described how entangled his haiku became with Bashō's as Kevin brought back the promised shots—plus one—carried in both hands like scorpions. Scarifying. Tattooing. Pagan fire, Johnny Jameson Irish.

"This is my blood of the New Testament which is shed for many," Kevin intoned, holding his shot glass in both hands overhead before he bore the brunt smoothly down his throat. We drank in silence. Hickey's presence was soon forgotten as he nodded in and out of sleep. Beer and whiskey kept coming as Mulcahy's took on a boisterousness seldom experienced as the storm of the decade raged.

Johnny fought off the effects of the whiskeys to make his point by dropping onto the table an oversized journal he had concealed in his coat for that purpose. On the cover was a grainy, bear-looking individual with a drooping Nietzsche mustache and hair sprouting out of his nose and ears. He thumped his fist on the image.

"That's him!"

At that precise moment, the knob on the front door revolved weakly in turns and halts as the men at the bar flinched under their collars in anticipation. For the third time in ninety minutes, Mulcahy's prepared to be invaded by the blizzard's gusts and icy snows. When the door was finally fought shut, standing among them was an angel in a bright green ski costume with a red nose sticking out.

Kevin recognized his sister Mary Ellen immediately. He sat back, grinning like The Honeymooners was about to start. Johnny eyed the drama around the door with his fist on the man on the magazine cover. He made a fleeting attempt at nonchalance and took a seat with the knowledge that running over to her—all excuses and regrets for whatever grievance brought her there—was not an option. The men at the bar soon realized the female nature of the intrusion and offered condolence and protection against the unnatural cold and wetness. Women were uncommon in men's bars.

"Aw, Miss," and, "Yer half-frozen, ya poor thing," and similar expressions were uttered. Mr. Lawless, known for his kindnesses, gathered her shoulders to look into her face, the dear child. "Come over the radiator won't ya for the warmpth."

Due to the proximity of the heat, a face emerged from the white fur tufts of the sheltering hood.

"Where is the motherfucker?" she said. The man— although shocked to hear the question—had a good idea. I hustled over, sliding to a stop in front of her.

"Mary Ellen! Will you look at you?"

A sound came from inside her like the woeful call of a distant gull. I had promised to talk to Johnny about getting over himself and his obsessions—a task I had no idea how to accomplish. Her eyes snapped shut.

"THIS was in the mail when I got home."

She handed me an envelope returned "postage due" with Johnny's scent—the lying bastard—all over a submission to some sketchy literary magazine.

"Rejected by the Post Office before the editor could," she said.

He apparently submitted a story one week after swearing to take a vacation from anything to do with writing or trying to get anything published—for her. He swore to give his dreams of fame and bizarre affectations a three-month timeout to dedicate himself to his wife.

"Was it too much to ask, Denny? A few months to pay attention to me?"

I would have traded my soul to hold her in my arms for one minute.

"He promised to stop so's I could sleep without his banging his typewriter into the night, without ripped-out pages flying, and him cursing the risin' sun with us due at work in an hour, not to mention the endless goings on about being plagiarized by everybody. I don't care if he wrote the Old Testament—where is he?"

Johnny was on the drunk side of himself, so was unfearful of death. He snuck up behind me before peeking his head out. She hit him in the eye with a leaping fist he took to cheers from the bar.

"You lied to me. You son of a bitch. Nobody does that, Healy."

Steaming, we coaxed her to our table. Johnny caressed the poor knuckles of her right hand and petted her body through the bubbly skin of her snow clothing.

"Here, Honey Bear, have a little taste," he said as Kevin came laughing over with another round, plus one.

"Sis of ours! Look here what I got ya."

Among the resources he carried was a heavily whiskey-laced coffee under whipped cream, topped with a peaked splotch of crème de menthe.

"You know I hate that green shit," she said.

Kev licked it off before handing it over.

Mary Ellen and I dated on and off through our high school and early college years before she met Johnny. She had the requisite patience to deal with an immature specimen like myself, coming as she did from a wild family of primarily boys. It was her and her mother against a tribe of billy goats, and her father, a hard-ass homicide detective with a head like a sewer plate.

I played hockey with two of her brothers. I loved her abundantly and without remorse. She had a pug nose with flaming red hair hanging down. She would laugh out loud after we kissed if she liked it and wore a Mets cap indoors and out on weekends. She looked like the kind of girl who would make love in a baseball cap given the chance. Mary Ellen was in every wet dream I ever had.

I introduced her to Johnny before a hockey game in which he scored a pair of goals and three assists. He covered ice like windblown mist—strides effortless and sure, now long, now short and crisp, heel over toe like ice dancing with himself. If we were on the ice together, he would pass me the puck knowing where I was without looking.

While I was getting the top of my eyebrow stitched back onto my face in the ER, Johnny took her home, because he was my best friend.

Johnny being Johnny, Mary Ellen fell for him immediately,

and as she could put up with nearly anything—even Johnny's whirling weirdness—she sank madly in love. He was totally unaware of what was taking place. I didn't bother explaining how it made me feel. I didn't need hearing "What'a ya mean, Den?" from Johnny, who would only vaguely perceive the implications.

He would insist on giving her back, like she was a pet dog followed him home. It was better to move on, even if I never did. I warned each separately not to marry the other. I was their "Best Man."

After several more deliveries from the bar, Mary Ellen and Hickey sat in curious awe of each other at opposite sides of the table. Johnny picked up the thread where he left off as if nothing happened, because in his world nothing had. He told us about a story he was writing about a guy, Thomas Mooney, who is visited by famous writers every night; Joyce, Fitzgerald, Pound, more, come to him in his mirror to prolong their writing lives beyond death.

He writes what they tell him to become wildly famous. One night he wakes to find he is on the other side of the mirror looking out. Proust, with a black painted-on mustache, is pecking at Mooney's typewriter by candlelight, while Mooney scratches at the gray stuff on the mirror's insides.

"I call it 'Mirror of Madness,'" Johnny said.

"Then I found this in a Brit literary rag about this Serbo-Croatian psycho-fantasy novelist." He ruffled through wet pages to point out a photo of a guy sucking on a Sherlock pipe the size of a tree stump.

"A Borislav guy. This friggin' thief! Writes about a struggling young writer named Darko, who's stuck in a cycle of literary metempsychosis."

"Metem-what?" Kevin asked, smiling at his sister, who did not smile back.

"Metempsychosis. Nitwit! Souls migrating into other

bodies. Dead genius-writers inhabit him—reincarnate into him —writing in his head while he sleeps. Darko copies it down each morning as if he thought of it himself."

"Johnny, Johnny, your mind is leaking," Kevin said. "You miss hockey. You miss hitting the puck with your head."

"I don't understand a word you're saying. Probably literary Tourette's," said Eddie.

"Johnny, I'm sorry. I get your point, but you're running full speed into yourself as usual," I said loud enough for Mary Ellen to hear. Hickey looked over, stark awake on his stool. I shrugged. He turned to Johnny to herald a sweeping declaration of lavish prescience.

"FLIP IT!" he shouted. He tried to stand.

"Make your Mooney character, your tortured hero, dictate to the great authors in THEIR magic mirrors what to write in THEIR timeless, precious classics. He's the sweeping hinge of literary civilization to illuminate the world! Sowing the seeds of the written word from horizon to horizon."

Hickey was a madman in his ear. Johnny was enthralled.

"He's the hot finger of Hermes up the noses of the great masters from Homer to Dickens. From Euripides to Uncle Remus. Call it 'Ghost Writer in the Sky.' And if they don't have mirrors, have him drop down their chimneys like Santy Claus."

Mary Ellen was drinking her whiskeys neat while I directed her thinking to the ferocity of the storm and the creatures sheltering in the nooks, spandrels, and perches unseen outside—spiders, mice, tiny huddling wrens.

Johnny took Hickey with two stools to the back room. This was bound to be good. I drifted closer. Hickey was on about the simultaneity of memory and the mutual penetration of opposites shook in a bag with eternal recapitulation, and other meta-philosophical delights.

"And that, Johnny Boy, is your hero! He's Diogenes

prancing with a lamp in one hand and his dick in the other. He's the guy atop the Tower of Babel cheering on the crowd to 'tell it like it is!'"

Hickey waddled back for another beer, leaving Johnny to figure it out, but I knew he would throw himself immediately into the work—the romance of such toil and suffering was irresistible. But there was also zero chance of coherence or success, so I joined him at the table to provide useless company. All I got was a nod and a peek into his notepad.

Between what I overheard and what he had already written, I knew Johnny had Hickey's "Ghost Writer" story mostly plotted. His re-envisioned Mooney was now equipped to rampage across time to instruct and inspire any creature possessed by the spark to weave a story or scratch a mark on a cave wall or mountainside.

Mooney was a demigod, lighting the fire of literature to spread through humankind. Thus, the prophetic words and fragmentary ravings of humanity came into the brief light of recorded history. Johnny was poised to create Mooney dauntless and heroically handsome like himself. All things were possible.

But even if Mary Ellen awoke blacked-out of the night's events—which was likely—there was no way any story written under Hickey's spell had not been written by someone else; once upon a time in an "as if" land far away, or by infinite monkeys banging on infinite typewriters.

Hickey was more likely to have cribbed random ideas from whatever library reading room he was warming up in that day. Outside, the volume and intensity of snow and gales flattened the high features of the earth and houses over Bay Ridge, Bensonhurst, and Canarsie up and down the broken coast of western Long Island.

A wind-burst of frozen diamonds rattled against the front

window. We stared into the red neon glow. The wind and the snow blew intolerably bitter across the concrete benches over-looking the Narrows' black waters—had anyone been there.

I was about to say something I would regret when Hickey whacked his empty shot glass on the table, his body recoiling from a deep, supra-gastric belch. He looked around the table, leaned in.

"Last week, I myself wrote Richard III." he confided.

"What a prick!" Johnny's eyes remained fixed on the window. He had work to do. All our eyes focused on the window. Beyond, snow-capped pigeons dreamed of desert cliffs over the River Jordan.

Mary Ellen awoke past noon to a terrible head, innocent of the night before, with only vague perceptions of returned submissions, snowstorms, mystery tramps, and whiskeys. Johnny made her breakfast in bed for lunch. Although he renewed his promises to give his obsessions a rest, she was not happy to discover over the next weeks an unpleasant surge of poetic energy in Johnny that he combined with a Dadaist, madcap seriousness.

The situation was ridiculous. Was I helping my best friend get over his weird impulses and his doggo literary lunacies, or was I just smoothing things over until the next crisis, when maybe I could make a move on his wife, whom I adored? If so, where did that leave me? Not that I was any brand of moralist —just canceled out by ambiguity of thought and act. I decided to do nothing.

More distressing in the real world was that unfounded territorial tension soon developed between Mary Ellen and me over withholding vital information about Johnny's all-consuming new project. Our paths would cross in the streets with steely indifference, or we would take pains to avoid each other altogether.

Once, I saw her swinging her arms down Fifth Avenue directly at me. Rather than trying to slide by, I crossed the street where we bumped into each other in the act of mutual evasion. It was obvious we were making matters worse, although I presumed her situation was far more serious—Johnny was her husband. I hunched my shoulders and opened my palms to indicate I was unarmed and ready to yield the field. She put her hands on mine until we felt safe to give little smiles. I took her to Marby's Ice Cream Shoppe on the side of the street we were originally walking on. There we gave up what we knew.

Johnny spent Saturdays at the main branch of the Brooklyn Public Library. Mary Ellen said he would return in the evening with books from the antiquities room and an eclectic selection from everywhere else.

I confessed to remembering, on the rare nights he spent in Mulcahy's, Johnny said nothing except he was "working on it," which was a vast departure from his usual running on about his transcendentalist thinking or his ghostly plagiarisms.

In school, he stared out the window at department meetings and ate lunch with his face in some tome or scratching in his notebook. My second thoughts about "Ghost Writer" seemed justified as months passed without word of his progress. Mary Ellen and I continued our pleasant sessions at Marby's on Fifth. I wasn't complaining.

Nevertheless, I sought help from several people I knew in grad school. I asked one guy, who was a psych wonk, about Johnny's reverse-plagiarizing delusions and odd airs. The guy said he never heard of it specifically, but delusions were common and often florid in bipolar and psychotic people.

"He could simply be plagiarizing these guys himself—either consciously or unconsciously. If it's the former, that's one thing; if the latter, that's another. That he feels the plagiarizing is reversed isn't good."

"Yeah. I thanked the guy."

Johnny was not your average amnesiac nor nutjob. Then again, maybe Johnny really was crazy. I sought out an acquaintance in anthropology. It was a case of, he said, "the invisible hand tipping the scales."

I bought the guy a coffee.

"Only JH's good stories are plagiarized, right?"

"Right." I could see where this was going. Eventually he launched into his judgement: "He insinuates himself into the particularly successful category of immemorial literature by occasionally writing good stories. If anybody writes a good story, they have a fair chance of having it already written by someone from the hallowed past, right?"

This guy was ready to go off the rails, so I said, "Right," and, "Thanks so much."

But he lit a cigarette and was blowing out a thin, slow stream of smoke to prepare for an unhurried exegesis, toward the end of which he finally concluded, "If, let's say, he writes bad stories, they receive little attention. He might even vet them in his mind before conceiving them.

"While if he writes a truly great poem, let's say, odds are there will be a Whitman or Frost poem like it to whatever degree it is. Sprinkle in a touch of 'cognitive dissonance'—I assume he 'wants' to write like Whitman—and there you have your friend."

Well, I suppose. I spoke to Johnny about both encounters.

"What did you expect them to say?" he asked.

Later that summer, Johnny stuck a copy of the final draft of Ghost Writer down my pants as we pinballed laughing off each other and the door frame coming out of Mulcahy's at closing. I hadn't seen him this cocky—ever.

I skimmed it streetlight to streetlight walking home alone through the low streets and alley cats. I read it several times over the next days. It was like being in on the Big Bang of human literature, but almost impossible to crack. Maybe that was the point.

The next time we got together was after freshman baseball tryouts. We walked in total silence below the heights of Bay Ridge, through playing fields and parklands in an essentially treeless plain but for juvenile maples crucified to wooden posts along the pathways by the Park Department.

Along with his gear, he carried a thirty-four-ounce Louisville Slugger bat he used as a prehistoric walking stick. He augmented the beginnings of a full, black beard with deep, hooded eyes. I took it Johnny was promoting a new persona, which was not a good idea. I saw in his duffel bag he was reading Pound and Homer. A bad brew. More importantly, I feared he was still conferring with Hickey about his completed story, which would confuse him even more than he already was.

It was best he work naturally through these phases, but he was overdue for intervention from his best friend.

"You might as well tell me. You eventually will," I said. He continued to walk to the thump of the bat, then stopped.

He said, "Ghost Writer." That was it.

We continued to walk in silent synch with each thump until I could take it no longer, stopped, and shouted, "So?"

"So? So, nobody wrote it, not just me, or everybody wrote it, which is the same thing. For all I know, everyone stole it from everybody else. I reread and reread it, until it just undid—nothing but snakes eating each other's tails."

"Yeah, I noticed."

He had apparently written himself into the aorta of something that refused to stop bleeding. We stood on the path. He played with the heft of the bat. The reeling of the last cicadas in the bushes hushed. He took an abrupt skip-step to underhand heave his ashplant bat as high as he could into the darkening scarlet and slate gray sky. The bicameral brain was centuries away. He was pre-Iliad, Agamemnon's great-great-grandfather.

The bat spun knob over trademark where the highest trees peaked. Several bystanders and I looked at him, the bat, then back, and then forth. Pigeons on apartment building ledges along the heights leaned forward. At apogee, its upward moment of inertia having been reached—if there is such a thing—the lumber rotated clockwise around itself like a bicycle wheel in the sky. It started down. Johnny studied it, arms at his side, his breath suspended, observing the natural truth of it.

At the perfect moment, as the bat whirled overhead, his right hand secured the handle, followed by the barrel, which flogged him across the center of his face, knocking him stone still on the grass, where he remained obtuse to the earth, the blood throbbing like pulsing worms from the bridge of his nose. He did not say why Mary Ellen left.

I stayed at his place to make sure he washed and ate. At the same time, I made the critical decision to go all out to fix Johnny's delusions and deficiencies, instead of half-assed asking around and documenting the loose ends. If I couldn't forget Mary Ellen—and I couldn't—then really helping her husband and my best friend was at least something. Anything was something.

Three months after the Louisville Slugger episode, I got Johnny to work on his first assured, crib-proof work of nonfiction, The Mystery Tramp: The Life and Times of Alfred

Hickey. It was the one project I could get him to do, although I knew it was a gamble bringing Hickey back into the picture.

I convinced Hickey to give me the rights to the ragtag pages he called his memoirs for a tent, a camping stove, a three-volume edition of Paradise Lost, which he probably sold after parading around with it, and a one-way train ticket to Florida to fuck off. I gave Johnny a writing schedule which he followed as if a child.

He was in a pathetic state, but the result was magical. A mixture of dubious fact and pure nonsense—half poem, half gothic horror. The Brooklyn Eagle gave it a hometown review. Johnny ended up with an agent and a modest two-book deal. Mystery Tramp made Hickey the cock of the bums for months, although he was supposedly in Tampa.

Mary Ellen came back. She thanked me with a smile and an ice cream at Marby's.

They moved into a semi-better apartment on Shore Road with a view of the Upper Bay and the ball fields. He became a minor celebrity at the high school where he continued to coach and teach to maintain his military deferment. Occasionally, Johnny showed at Mulcahy's for a bull session with the gang, although his free time was sparse. Johnny focused on magical biography, a genre he helped popularize with his new collaborator—me—who kept introducing fresh, dubious protagonists.

A succession of books followed about men and women shrouded in urban myth: people who proved the city was a dirty, corrupt, and hopeless place where cheap sainthood and questionable celebrity were always around the next corner—people like Jake Teitelbaum: the Stickball Babe Ruth. Thousands saw him play, but little was known of the man—until Johnny came along. What couldn't be determined, he made up.

"It was his word against mine. And he didn't say anything."

Johnny's next offering was The Saint of Attica Prison, an

unauthorized biography of Salvador Bocce, a mobster I initially researched from the prison archives and the NYC papers. Doing life for racketeering and homicide, he wrote inspirational poetry and hymns for the incarcerated soul, and performed undocumented miracles that Johnny documented: unexplained cures, last-second clemencies, and saintly apparitions in solitary confinement cells.

Healy's depictions of urban folk legends were so lyrically drawn their veracity seldom came under scrutiny. Critics and readers assumed they were largely wishful thinking spackled with guesswork. For Johnny, these half-baked character studies were harvesting the lowest of low-hanging fruit, yet they provided a way out of his literary rabbit hole.

In the Healy pipeline was Mole: The Story of Juliette Lamb, a blind albino who gave birth to a dozen children and engaged countless lovers in abject poverty from birth to death in an underworld hobo colony, layers below the twisting NYC subway system.

I always held out hopes for Mary Ellen, but she was content enough, in a resigned, hopeless way. Me? I was nothing. The baseball season was over. My classes were barely decent—I liked a couple of kids. My life was Thursday nights at Mulcahy's, almost always without Healy, which was okay.

While Johnny worked on the middle chapters of Mole, Mr. Mulcahy passed from one world into the next where Mrs. Mulcahy had passed previously. He was more than willing to go.

Johnny and Mary Ellen sent a large, costly flower arrangement to the wake, which was soon lost among the common tears and stories, the jokes and ha-ha lies of the rare ould times.

A hearse, along with a parade of cars with headlights softened by the spring sky over Jamaica Bay, carried Mr. Mulcahy like the body of Achilles along the Belt Parkway into the former frontier lands of Queens. There wasn't a share of clay for a soul to sleep in peace anywhere in Brooklyn. Miles of rocky earth and untenable piles of broken boulders left by the ice-age moraine near the Midtown Tunnel provided proprietary opportunities for the creation of fifteen cemeteries, with abundant room for the departed of all denominations and non-beliefs.

Later, we made the sad journey back to Brooklyn to the bar, where there were microscopic triangular ham and cheese sandwiches. I called Johnny, but no one answered.

A few weeks later, while walking home alone from Mulcahy's at closing, I knocked into Johnny inside a curtain of sewer gas near my crummy apartment where I now lived alone. He wore a droopy 1920s newsboy's cap, possibly inherited from his grandfather.

"Mary Ellen's gone," he said.

I'd heard it before. Nonetheless, something inside fluttered. We walked toward the faint lights of Eighty-Sixth Street. The Bum's Rush was open until 3 a.m. We looked at and away from each other, both in the flesh and in the mirror behind the bottles, thinking of what to say. Deep-rooted shit was coming at us through the walls.

"I didn't finish half of Mole before I lost all sense of her, Juliette. You know what?"

"Yeah, probably."

"I started to feel like Tom Mooney, my old 'Mirror of Madness' guy, with words flying out of me onto pages told by ghosts in an imaginary mirror who wasn't me."

"Anyone I know in the mirror?"

"Stephen Crane was in the mirror, figuratively speaking. He was our age when he wrote Maggie. Different times, same place—except one's above, and the other in the depths of the subway. Juliette started being Maggie. The tone and plot got close, close enough to be considered, you know, Crane's. Or Mooney's—which was really me once removed."

"You're saying you were plagiarized by yourself. And Crane."

"You could say."

Johnny couldn't help what side of the mirror he was at, but I bet no one ever wrote a Crane story nor a Bashō poem better than Johnny, nor stories superior to de Camp and a half dozen others ever wrote. He was an antenna without a dial, at risk of picking up artistic discharges and story arcs back and forth from past and arcane places. Whether he was more evolved than the rest of us, or steps removed in the pre-human past, didn't matter to him.

He put on his slouch cap, presented a draft of the first half of his tangled Mole/Maggie mess which he seemed proud of, like it was a trick before the royal court he performed just for me. We headed out the door. He walked with slapstick languor into the night, up Third Avenue toward the bay.

In the morning in my apartment, I stood before a photo of Johnny and Mary Ellen on their wedding day, with me standing next to him, half out of the frame. What kind of story was my life? I called her at her parents' place.

"I saw Johnny," I said.

"So?"

"So, listen..."

Saturday afternoon, we had a little picnic at Cannon Park while her hair hissed at me in the breeze. I brought the Mole/Maggie draft that she wanted nothing to do with. She didn't move when I touched her face. She'd moved back with her parents; her and Johnny's apartment was impossible to keep on one salary.

The long way back to her parents' place brought us along streets with the moon following treetop to treetop. I kept the things I saw and felt close inside, thinking what I'd tell her if there would ever be a time.

Johnny had vanished—from his teaching job as well. The totality of his leaving was not lost on us. Over the next months, Mary Ellen and I "saw each other." We went to the movies or cheap Off-Off-Broadway shows. Johnny's existence never came up, which was worse than if it had. We caught Mets games. Sometimes I stayed over at her parents' place on the sofa. I'd have breakfast with the Dolans before heading off. We did Marby's.

What was her life like without Johnny? I could guess. No lonely epiphanies nor tinkling bells of fictional sacraments unheard. No Keats nor "Sheik of Araby" to ignore her for weeks, nor the pain of being unintentionally lied to.

Johnny's life had been so like a personal circus, he seemed to be there when he had already torn down the tents and left town, taking the elephants and tigers with him. Life for me was her. Flowers were stolen from gardens. She discovered me staring at her when I thought she wasn't looking. Once she closed her eyes to complete a slow-growing yawn across her face. I kissed her nose when she finished. For every rainbow I found reflected in a mud puddle, I wrote a poem I didn't give her.

Six months into our on-the-verge affair, I made a discovery. Hickey was back, or had never left. So was Johnny.

There existed in Brooklyn a spy network that worked like airborne spores of small, unverified truths:

Nobody knows nothing. All's I know is, someone heard from someone else Hickey was seen feeding pigeons in Owl's

Head Park; fellas believed they heard fellas in the Harbor Bar say he comes sometimes schnorring for handouts.

There were Johnny rumors, too. A local bookstore owner I knew let slip Johnny's circumstances. After quitting teaching, the whole time Mrs. Healy and I were seeing each other, her husband was living in a downtown YMCA, writing all day and surviving off the feeble royalties from his sketchy biographies.

I envisioned him meeting Hickey for literary salons in the bars and flophouses around the downtown underworld.

It was senseless to hunt for Hickey, and I wasn't sure I wanted to find Johnny, but I left a message where I knew he would get it.

We met in the little park under the Brooklyn Bridge by an expressway stanchion, listening to tires sizzle overhead in the early morning's foggy dew. Johnny knew everything—what little there was—about Mary Ellen and me, I was sure. He never brought it up. He probably thought I was doing him a favor. Johnny and I never knew what to say to each other anyway.

As the situation hovered, Johnny's black hair quivered across his eyes like a horse's tail. He was up to something. There was no sense asking.

"Tell Mary Ellen be good to herself. And, you know, Denny, you too."

He took off up Tillary Street. I called Mary Ellen from a pay phone to tell her what happened, even though it was nothing.

"So?" she said.

Soon, we got real Johnny news. A new curiosity hit local bookstores, an absurdist roman-à-clef novel, A Knight in Brooklyn, based roughly on Don Quixote by a local writer: Johnny Healy.

Set in 1971, Johnny's characters roamed Brooklyn like 1600s Spain.

The ultimate insult depended on whether you perceived yourself in it or not, and whether you thought that a good or bad thing. I was totally Sancho Panza.

Many of the important characters from the neighborhood were unwilling parodies of themselves. Mary Ellen was the Raggedy Ann Dulcinea love interest. The Windmill might have been Mulcahy's. Hickey was a replica of himself as Quixote's horse, making pompous orations and gigantisms like a stallion out of Gulliver's Travels. Mary Ellen had had enough. Me? I was happy to oblige.

Back at my place, early Saturday, I started gathering my Johnny Story tangle into a big canvas bag, along with everything of Johnny I had back to high school: photos, poems, stories, drafts, team trophies, noetic ramblings, manu-scribbles.

A few hours later, Mary Ellen surprised me by joining me to put in her share of knickknacks, including her wedding ring. We pulled the string taut. I wrote The Collected Works and Eternal Past of Johnny Healy across the front with a black marker, and we signed it.

There was a spot off the lower harbor where the Hudson folds into the Atlantic, next to the ball fields and courts filling up with kids. On the barrier rocks, brown crabs scuttled across skeins of seaweed in the surf, expecting the morning to go exactly as the past two hundred million years had.

We swung the bag between us to gather momentum carefully, like we had Moses in a basket.

"Into the snot-green, great, sweet mother sea I commend your soul," I said softly, as in a prayer.

Double plagiarized—Joyce and Swinburne. We hurled it into the tide, barely clearing the rocks. It hesitated, grew darker green as it drifted, and sank toward the Verrazzano Bridge and the open Atlantic.

We both had things to do. I went straight back to my apartment, turned on the Mets game for noise, and dealt with the dishes by actually washing them. The curtains were covered with dust. I shook them out the back window, mostly into my face. I used the blue stuff and newspapers to clean the windows like my mom. I felt there was a rat behind the sink and investigated. I threw out all my clothes but a pair of pants, some shirts, and a ball of underwear. I wanted everything different. Mostly me.

I found a copy of A Knight in Brooklyn that escaped earlier pillaging and took it downstairs to the curb to finish. Johnny did a great job turning himself into the Knight of the Doleful Countenance, blustering and rampaging, complicating the world's already insoluble problems with his disguises and theatrics. Wonderful, Johnny. I threw it into the trash can.

Back upstairs, I reworked a poem I'd started the day before, about a rainbow in a mud puddle. I was Sancho Panza, not a poet. It wasn't good. I fell asleep on the sofa with my poem between the cushions. Maybe I'd give it to Mary Ellen, if she was still talking to me.

In the morning, Mary Ellen let herself into my apartment building past the vestibule's tin mail slots with tenants' nameplates. I still don't know how she got in without a key. I heard her clomp up the first flight, dragging a military-style duffel bag.

On the second-floor landing, she passed the doors of the Adelmans, Pudlucks, and Della Donnes; thump-thump-thump up the next flight past the McWeeneys, Jasinkiewiczs, and the Midget Marys on the next landing; then up the final flight where I stood in my doorway in my shorts between the Zalooms and Finkelsteins, who were surely awake.

"I wasn't expecting company. I thought you'd never make it up the stairs."

"Dickhead." I grabbed her bag. It was heavy. She looked around the apartment. I was glad I did the dishes.

"I gotta use the head," she said. Mr. Dolan was a Marine.

She came out wearing only a Mets cap.

"Here's the deal," she said. "We wrestle to see where I sleep. If I win, I sleep on the sofa. If you win, I assume I sleep with you."

She turned her cap backwards.

"Want me to let you win?" she said.

"Na. I'll take my chances."

The Collected Works and Eternal Past of Johnny Healy reached the Atlantic that night. Or it was caught on the barrier rocks to pitch and to roll in the tide. Either way, it had already been written by someone else. Or soon would be.

The Story of Jimmy Gray

"What the people believe is true."
—Nanabush, Son of the West Wind,
Grandson of the Moon

Victory Memorial Hospital
Bay Ridge, Brooklyn, NY
[1968 — 1975]

I was a story I told myself.

My body required mechanical help with inputs and outputs, causes and effects—the purpose of one function needed to be fitted to the function of a higher purpose, from swerve of nerve to bend of bone, synapse to neuron across the junctions electric. Body shifts, reflex tests, muscle pulls were performed. Others asked questions, neither understood nor answerable.

"Who is president?"

"One plus one is...?"

"What is your name?"

As my broken brain stitched itself together without me, my emerging mind sniffed like a timid mouse among the gears and hydraulics for hints.

I performed inventories: self-awareness—check; internal language mechanisms—check; free will—none; movement—none; operational contact with eyelids, mouth, arms, legs, hands, thirst, time, ice hockey, erotic desire, sunsets and rises, phases of the moon—negative. What was my name?

Yet a slipstream of reciprocity existed between me and the world. Although I could not touch, sometimes I could feel my fingers caressed. And while I could not cry out, I noticed the borders between silence and sound, distinguished intimate melodies from riled waves in the air of someone passing by—the way fronds of a fern might bend to a breath of wind.

This lonesome dance of the senses became dreaming and dreaming proxy doing. I dreamed I was e. e. cummings. I dreamed I was a bird turned to the breeze on a bough. I dreamed there was a land of islands, mists, and rivers, and I went to it over a deep ocean.

Lacking terrain, it struck me the island was not real, yet I contented myself with what was there. With me was something like a spirit or the oldest man ever lived, who dreamed with me, which made him as real as anything else. He said his name was Nanabush—Son of the West Wind, Grandson of the Moon.

He said my name was Me or my name was George Washington. He bought smoke for us to breathe. When we exhaled, we made stories. Each breath a scene, each loop a memory, each turn a dream on a great river.

He told a story of a spirit asleep like me in a place that was not him, who dreamed of ceremonies and drumming and charms, waterfalls and stars, fire and more.

He said, "Me, it was dark even so. It exists nothing only He, the Great Spirit. Dreamed up the Grand Fathers and Mother Moon."

His story was long with fantastical details. The crux was: the earth was covered with water, a large tortoise raised up to become land where a tree grew. Out of its roots a sprout bore the first man and woman. The story seemed told in real time over centuries, with strangers come over the sea intent to kill the earth and the Common People. There was no rush.

When he stopped, he gave me the pipe and said:

"Tell the 'Story of Me' to find who Me is. Begin where you remember on Flowing River."

I remembered zero. We blew puffs into the gulf to find a thread into my story. I went to the Flowing River with no notion, so I started with my last inkling of the last day before... this.

I told "The Story of Me"—as foreign as someone else's life told in a history book. My words revealed that at eighteen I was reunited with the love of my life, Ms. Caprice DiMaggio, after a three-year absence for approximately a month of blissful co-existence.

Of our time together, I could report few concrete details. I understood there was a lot of necking during those weeks, but this was probably more deduced in mind than remembered from life. In those days, it was well known Catholic teens did a lot of deep kissing and grinding on each other like dogs until we wanted to get married or shoot ourselves.

What happened next was as swift a descent into my present unfortunate state as I could have imagined. I came to understand Caprice had a girlfriend, Sissy, who was my friend Dennis Hackett's sister. There was reason to support—after I was verbally abused and dumped by my angel Caprice—Sissy co-opted me for her boyfriend like one acquires a used hamster from a pet store.

"You're your own worst enemy, Jimmy Gray," Sissy said.

It was early fall. It was 1965, and I was Jimmy Gray.

Pope Paul VI had just celebrated Mass in Yankee Stadium. U.S. Marines repelled an attack by Viet Cong forces at Da Nang Airport. Three hundred years previously, over a hundred Lenape Common People seeking shelter across the "North" River from New Amsterdam were slaughtered by Dutch soldiers.

I can't find my wallet. "If it had teeth, it would bite you," she said.

She relied on clichés and canards to pinpoint my flaws. Sometimes I thought she was talking about herself, she had it down in such analytic detail. She felt she was doing me a favor,

as my girlfriend, to chip away the rough edges—that I was ore to
be smelted into something serviceable; that this was what made
her my girlfriend.

"You do everything by the seat of your pants, you know?"

Yes, I knew.

"You're a disaster waiting to happen."

She told me why. It was because I didn't write down things
I needed to remember. I treated these boilerplate bromides as
backhand validations.

If my wallet had teeth, what? Nothing. A wallet with teeth
would be as unlikely to bite me as a glass of water with teeth. I
took these remarks as hall passes to avoid my real problems,
which I preferred to keep to myself. But when she said these
things, her face, where her cheeks and eyes met, got
compressed and wrinkly like she was squinting into the sun.
For some reason, even though it made her look slightly sour like
a talking weasel—and I knew she was trying to be serious—I
could spin her around until she became hysterical laughing. Of
course, I never did.

"Jimmy Gray, do what you believe, not what others want,"
she said as her glasses hopped up her nose. She wore glasses.
Very contemporary, with large silver frames.

Sometimes Sissy's glasses made me want to be extra nice in
compensation. It wasn't a pity thing, exactly. It was complex.

Yes, I wanted to make up for the glasses, which, let's face it,
weren't that attractive. They made me want to see beyond
banging my cheekbone into her frames or figuring out where
my nose went when I kissed her.

On the other hand, her eyes looking out, magnified behind
the lenses, had a positive effect on me because she had really
nice eyes. Like a pair of blue gourami swimming around two
little fishbowls.

The sexiest thing was, she'd kiss me with her glasses on,

mostly, but if she took them off, if she put them on a picnic blanket or into her pocket, or let them drop—I'd get a lump in my throat I'd have forever.

A ghostly black-and-white seagull—possibly flapped out from a round trip to the Caribbean with the family—squatted with its poor hollow wings aching on a streetlamp outside the parking lot of Sunset Park Pool at the corner of Sixth Avenue and Forty-Fourth Street.

It was an unnaturally hot Indian summer Saturday. Sissy Hackett and I banked under the gull on our bikes heading for a midday swim, then up to Shore Road to relax on the heights where we might find a breeze with autumn in it.

At the pool, we went to our sex-specific locker rooms—two high halls built during the Depression where we changed under murals of mythological sea demons and ceiling dolphins blowing spews of water filled with flying fish.

High-pitched screams and laughter in several languages frolicked in feedback loops onto the benches below, like the rumbling of giants. I suspected chlorine and rumors of the proximity of children in the air before I saw the pool.

The sun shimmered off a thousand impressionist waves. Sissy, her rusty red hair black after a nose-pinched jump, was blind without her glasses at the four-foot marker. She hunched against the splashes of invisible children she heard nearby. I dove to her around lovers, grandparents, and red-eyed kids of indefinite religions and colors, curated by chance and necessity from every brink of the earth.

Three hours later, we pedaled our bikes with rolled towels and wet bathing suits under our seats across Fourth Avenue and down Thirty-Ninth Street toward warehouses and the docks along the Brooklyn waterfront.

Breukelen: The Broken Land. Dutch.

Lenapehoking: Land of the Common People. Lenape.

It was hard work along Third Avenue between cars and trucks, bumping into traffic lights with nothing but bus stops, delis, bars, chain-link garbage cans, and apartment buildings with first-floor stores overflowing onto the sidewalks.

We wheeled, psychedelic, down Seventy-Fifth Street through shadows of sun-splotched leaves. Hawthorns and elms. Everywhere, maple trees shed seeds with fuses set to go off next spring. Children called them poly-noses because they stuck them on their noses like clothespins to look like parrots or baby rhinos. I lurched at one as we rode through a squadron helicoptering in the wind.

Brownstones with stone stairs stood shoulder to shoulder, rowhouse style on each side of the street to share laughter, nightmares, and screams of love and anger. On top of the stoops were concrete lion planters with a geranium apiece that smelled like cat pee, depending on the season, with a family in the basement that had underground views of trash cans.

Stoep: Dutch. Wikhatuwikaon: Lenape.

I saw myself. I scanned a car window with Me in it as we waited at an intersection. It was Jimmy Gray. We pedaled into the canopied darkness of Colonial Road. I wheeled next to her.

"Do you suppose living things have souls that come back after death?" I asked.

"What do you mean? Come back where?"

"My parakeet Edgar died, is all. I buried him in a jar. I almost cried. I didn't think of crying when they buried Uncle Mike."

There were ebbs and there were phases to bike-riding conversations to do with relative distances, the breath span of comment to response, the apprehension of sudden movements, quantum rhythms, worldly and otherworldly. When one spun the other spun a second before or after or both together to make it impossible to know who did what, when, or why—which was a beautiful and mysterious thing.

"Not like the bird dying was a tragedy, only worse. Like finding somebody's pet cat dead in the street. The animal didn't know it was coming—death, I mean—doesn't understand it's even possible. It gets run over chasing a leaf or something and next—nothing. It gets buried if it's lucky or kicked into a sewer. It doesn't even know it's gone."

"Yeah, you cried. Which is only natural," she said.

No living thing but us seemed to be down Colonial Road that wasn't theoretically in an apartment or car, but the hidden fecundity passed with invisible souls at bicycle speed—in trees, sewers and backyards, underground and between the cracks—until we were joined by a barking dog raising dust under a sumac tree behind a hurricane fence.

I pulled to her right and stood on the pedals of my stripped-down English Racer. Sissy rode a big red Schwinn—hard to move, fat tires, broad handlebars with an oddly small, silver ringer she worked, brrrring, brrrring with her thumb. She angled in front, eyes over her shoulder, and wiggled her butt.

"I kind'a like the idea of animal souls," she said.

We leaned into Ninety-Fifth Street past Saint Patrick's Church and satellite bars: Kelly's for the Men's Holy Name Society on Tuesday nights, the Harbor Bar for the bite Saturday night before the hair-of-the-dog Sunday morning after Mass, and Mulcahy's for beers and balls without provocation. There was more sky.

We were confined and connected to each other in the gears, the distances between, the breathing, and the words of "The Story of Me." Sissy Hackett and Jimmy Gray in space and time down the sloping heights toward a street we could never reach, faithful to the paradox of Zeno's arrow, toward the flatlands of Brooklyn and Coney Island.

Konijn Eiland: Dutch. "Rabbit Island." Wichquawanck: Lenape.

A suspension of narrative rapport occurred while Sissy and I spun our wheels between Ninety-Fifth Street and the retreating universe. Nothing was possible until there was the distinct pong of smoldering herbs—hemp or sage. Nothing could be gleaned nor spoken in my story, nor could I tell it, until Nanabush came into the moment.

"The arrow of 'Story of Me' is stuck," he said. He blew a beam of smoke into the scene.

I forgot, or forget, or will forget I was telling my story to Nanabush across the ever-cycling river. My story was out of tense. Was I telling it in the present about the past? Or in the past explaining to my present self what already happened? Or was I inventing a story to become Me at some future date?

The two figments of my story, Sissy and I, were lost in every relative respect.

"Why is that?" Nanabush wished to know. "Why Zeno arrow can't hit target?"

I told him Zeno's arrow can never hit its target, because "it has to go halfway, then halfway again, and again... forever."

We applied the pipe to this problem. We sat with foreheads pressed against each other until Nanabush's words came out in foggy trails, word by word, in this order:

"Reason story go halfway, Zeno think too much. Arrow lack courage waiting in air for time catch up or distance slide back. Either way. Launch words. Okay. Link with Grandmother Moon and Father Sun, finish Story of Me."

The Schwinn and the English Racer parted and rejoined many times in the lull of the afternoon. I had something to say that had difficulty coming out.

Edgar had dragged himself by his beak along the bottom of his cage through black-and-white droppings like tiny confections, through piles of seed husks, green tail and white downy under-feathers trying to get to his swing, infinitely above.

The bird's eyes tried to understand, I wanted to tell Sissy. I wished I could have picked him up, held him close against my cheek, and snapped his neck like a wishbone for his senseless trying—for his not-understanding to be over. But I couldn't. Then I could.

"People see a light before they die," she said, when she caught up. "Maybe animals too, probably. People who come back say they were drawn to it but pulled away. As if someone called them back. It's a common occurrence."

She said this like an anthropologist discussing primitive belief systems, leaning over her handlebars. It took out whatever kindness there might have been behind what she said.

"Yes. Edgar saw the light. Uncle Mike saw Banquo's ghost leaning against a streetlamp lighting a cigarette saying, 'Going my way?' If anything, it's the light disappearing they saw. It's life's taillights. It's the sudden strangeness of shutting down into darkness, into... into what, Sissy? Does it really matter if the light's coming or going?"

I didn't think she heard what I said about the light, because she was pumping hard to catch up as we got to Shore Road. We found a bench in the shade of a sycamore tree, shed of brown bark down to the green under-skin with its leaves rattling at the breeze. The sidewalk was free of mothers pushing strollers, kids, and lost souls, so I put my arm around her to listen to the tree, just in case. I felt like holding her. Maybe she would take her glasses off.

Sissy was impossible to rate. With girl inflation due to intangibles—let's say you were fond of red hair, or pug noses, or went for girls with broad, gummy smiles—she was super. She had nice breasts, for example. Any breasts would be fine by me, but if sculpted onto a thin girl, her breasts would be amazing.

She was perhaps slightly plumpish. But her greatest asset was theoretical: her womanhood.

The promise of humanity was in her, hidden inexplicably in her body, a gateway through which billions and billions of baby boys and girls clamored to enter the world to have their hearts broken. She had something important to say—I could tell by the swell of birds looking down from the trees. She took her time.

I was in the recovery stages of a hockey stick to the mouth that puckered my right upper lip over the bottom. I practiced the look from various angles in windows and bathroom mirrors.

A teammate helped me cut the sutures out with special scissors he borrowed from his mother. I thought the lip made me Hollywood handsome after a movie fistfight. But Sissy saw it as the permanent mark of the Devil. From my perspective, it was great to kiss her with the puffy lip. It was kisses times two, kisses squared, at the intersection of Pain Street and Pleasure Avenue.

"Why do you play hockey?" she asked, like it was evidently ridiculous.

"Hockey? What do you mean?"

"I don't know, maybe so's not to have to kiss me with your lip hanging off your face."

"I like kissing you."

It was a dopey thing to say. She twisted a rope in her hair.

"That's not the point," she said. "I think you want people to think you're a hard ass. You need stitches all over your face to show you're tough, so's you can pull them out with pliers like a savage. You don't have to pretend, Jimmy."

I wanted to tell her hockey was teaching me something profound, only I couldn't figure it out in enough sensible detail to explain what it was. She wasn't finished with me, spinning her hair now like the cotton candy man.

"Next, you'll be peddling your face around like some John Wayne wannabe in an Iwo Jima movie in the nearest mirror or auditioning for a Jimmy Cagney hoodlum film—'The Duke of Brooklyn'—in a shiny car hood. That's you." That was me.

"Let me ask you a question," I said, hoping to tease the conversation away from her favorite subject—me.

"What were the people called who lived along this river a thousand years ago?"

She knew not to bite, but she did. "What does that have to do with anything?"

"You're so into animal souls. They believed people and animals had souls that recycled. They checked out their newborns for signs whether they were dead relatives or family pets."

I must have been to the Brooklyn Museum in my recently obliterated past, I was so sure.

"They roved up and down around here for haven among the cold cliffs. Under freezing stars. Shucking mussels and oyster shells with the wolves howling. They spied the fires of other human beings along the bluffs and river's shelves and palisades."

So as not to seem inadequate in any way, she let her mind stop organizing in its customary manner to focus on the problem of the native people.

She said, "They called themselves... How do I know?"

"The Lenape! Their villages were on both sides of the river and the flatlands by the ocean. Artifacts were found right on this ridge. Drums and pottery. There were wolves and porcu-pines and bears, not here anymore—their souls included." Her eyes grew theatrically cool.

"Yes, of course. I must have misplaced my Lenape Indian guidebook."

The situation hovered. She was extremely sensitive about

herself. Her brother Dennis could tell how her demeanor was trending using a scale he instinctively envisioned. It was a curse, he said—a sixth sense about most people.

Dennis was always full of shit. He saw personalities as multidimensional models. His dad was a slotted cylinder.

His girl, Annette, had attitudes he plotted inside a pyramid. The base points were pathos, bathos, and the theory of relativity, with joy at its pinnacle. Somewhere within this chiseled space was Annette. If she was hovering near the top in the middle, the lower points were gravitationally not in effect, and she was playful as a puppy. Traveling down, she'd go grossly sentimental or dank between befuddled and subatomic. His kind of girl.

He said Sissy's attitudes and postures slid inside a slanting cube. I was not sure what that implied, and I wasn't sure Dennis did either, but the points inside must have been inestimable—not to mention what the niches were called, or where they were located. It was one of the things I loved about her. Her angled, fly-on-the-wall intensity inside the grid, longing for a breather on a borderline condition, up for a mandible rub on a dubious ledge, or upside down, talking to herself in fly across the wide rhombohedron universe.

I wasn't sure I wasn't in there with her. Maple seeds twirled in the gaps between the breezes above our heads, each on its course along the chain of life with a one-in-a-million hope of becoming half a sapling.

Sissy was sullen, projecting her wolf-like self over the iron fence upon the choppy blackness of the Narrows to experience once again the bitterness of the Lenape. It was the emptiest of the faces she had available. She trained a wide un-focus on the clouds. I plucked a poly-nose from the air to alter the mazy mood, broke it in half, peeled it at the seed head, and licked the sticky milk to adhere it to the tip of my nose.

"And besides," she said from deep inside, softening, knowing she had prevailed once again through the magic of passive aggression.

"And besides what?"

"Just besides."

She turned to me and saw my face waiting to hear what she had to say.

"You have a poly-nose on your nose," she said, like it was breaking news.

"A poly-nose?"

"Yes, a poly-nose, because it's like a parrot's nose—not because it belongs on yours."

"It must have fallen on my face from the sky or a maple tree."

No one could stay angry with a person wearing a poly-nose. Sometimes I felt about eight years old around her. She was fitting into herself as a grown woman while I was screwing around with poly-noses. But a poly-nose could be a powerful tool.

Looking out over one cleaves everything in sight in half—it puts a greenish-brown, unanticipated barrier in the middle of a person's life. Sissy's views were definitive and unalloyed. If she ever snuck up, "Good morning, Jimmy!" wearing a poly-nose, I'd suck her toes until she died laughing. If I were Jesus, I'd wear a poly-nose making the rounds, and hand them to followers as a sign of our new religion. I'd lick one on Peter's apostolic nose to found my Church. I'd say, "Someday, Pete, you may need to look down one of these to explain the Blessed Trinity to the Gentiles. Good luck."

She snorted, but smiled her smile, and turned her left hand inward to finger my shoulder like a woman playing a cello, as we looked over the fence into the harbor. And we were happy together among the maple trees' spinning children.

A bunch of guys we didn't know came our way in stern hostility along the sidewalk. It was getting dark. They looked identical, with quirky moves, cruising in black outfits. I knew not to do or say anything. I could tell, the way you can tell, they were from somewhere else. Red Hook or Bensonhurst. One got into us, sat down next to Sissy. He didn't say much either. Three others hung against the iron fence in studied nonchalance.

"Nice nose," the guy said. My chances for a tactical bluff were none.

"How much ya got on ya? I'm taking a survey," he said, leaning over Sissy. I shrugged. The guy smiled. The poly-nose unhinged.

"Nice boy like you on a bench with Ginger here must have a few bucks," he said.

He put his hand on her knee. I hated her fat, chubby knees. How she closed her eyes. How she persisted, latent on the bench, trying not to breathe. How I was in charge of her and her chubby knee.

"How about your skanky friend here? What's she got?" He squeezed her knee, looping his fingers up the inside of her thigh, looking into my eyes.

I had a left jab my father taught me. He only had a left jab, and that's all I had—fine for hockey pile-on, spin-around fights on the ice.

There wasn't anything to think about, so I stood up. What with Sissy, her thigh, and the skank business, I cut a left jab at his face that he ducked under. It was more a gesture than a punch. His smile grew oddly tight around the hinges. He blocked another obvious left, then threw roundhouse combos I slid between. He closed in, grappling, punching my ears and ribs, a mix of boxing and street jujitsu.

We began a painful dance. He raised his knee into my nuts

a few times, which I rode like a hobby horse. We settled into grunting choke holds and standing headlocks, his greasy hair in my face, and tripping moves to leverage the other over. I considered the ironies of what we were doing and the sharp stink of his black shirt.

We gazed into each other's eyes as we bounced off parked cars and park benches with our heads and shoulders in each other's arms. I saw for a split moment what looked like an unfocused Man-in-the-Moon float in front of my face. I launched my previously unavailing right fist into the moon.

There was something on his face he hadn't previously noticed. He stumbled back, probing his nose. Blood came dripping red between his fingers. Slow crimson dots splattered the street like a Jackson Pollock painting on the sidewalk. The others were on me before I could apologize. I hit the concrete.

What I lacked as a fighter, I made up for taking a beating. They kicked me with black Converse sneakers with white ovals on their ankles. I sang a song to myself to change the tone and interpretation of my situation. I sang a song the family used to sing when we were happy and us kids bounced in the back seat of the Buick. I used the song trick to distract me getting stitches or wringing out leg cramps. It was my dad's favorite.

Beautiful dreamer, wake unto me. Starlight and dewdrops are waiting for thee.

Well into it, one of them decided stomps on my head were appropriate, which compressed my face into the pavement of sandstone, clay, gypsum, and tiny, almost translucent yellow and white river stones. Folding into a warm place under the concrete street, I completed a last phrase.

Sounds of the rude world, heard in the day, lull'd by the moonlight have all pass'd away!

I thought I heard Moon Face singing with me and Sissy screaming—or perhaps all of us were screaming—until nothing was, except the moving away into the sidewalk, expanding into the elemental world. One of them stuck a knife into my left lung through my back ribs, like slipping a plug into a socket. It tasted sweet. Sleepy and sweet. Poly-noses spun. Sissy's glasses came off. It tasted warm and sleepy like my mother's milk. Nebula sweet.

I was at the end. I tried to find more things to say. Someone moved forward to cup the back of my head.

Nanabush blew smoke rings into the resolution of The Story of Me.

"Go Milky Way?" he asked. "Be star. Or want try person again? Find who you are next. Okay? This one not so good."

"Catholics don't believe in spirits reincarnating nor becoming stars," I said.

"Don't believe in Nanabush neither. Want come back two people? No problem for you."

"One, thanks. Will I remember Me?"

"You need tell story where river flows in circle with the next you to remember Me. No problem for you."

"Who was Me, anyway? Was Me Jimmy Gray?"

"If you want. You two seem hit it off. Want come back girl? Take your time. Not too long, okay?"

"Can I still be a star? In the Milky Way?"

"What the people believe is true," he said. "You find out soon enough."

The perimeter was empty. Nanabush drew a celestial hit from his pipe that sent embers into his eyes. He sat, criss-crossed, sparkling in the dark.

My eyes opened to a bank of milky fluorescent lights. The Story of Me was finally over. I said "Hello" to a person who hurried away as Jimmy Gray began to reboot.

There came a woman in a white uniform who asked, "Who is president?"

"Georgie Washington."

"What's your name?"

"Me! Or Jimmy Gray. Either or," I said, and people laughed.

Saigon had recently fallen to the People's Army of Vietnam, and Secretariat won the Kentucky Derby. The Common People had been removed from the Lenapehoking for well over two hundred years by then.

Soon, I was introduced to my parents, some friends, and a woman who said she loved me truly, times two, kisses squared. I had my concerns. I stared out the window into the Milky Way whose stars I could see as shadows on the streets.

My memories began from that moment, forward and backward in time, at twenty-six years old. I headed into the future and into the past, to enlighten the gaps and bridge the missing years at the dawn of "The Story of Jimmy Gray," both a tick ahead and a tock behind myself. *Tik-tok*. Dutch. Nèke. Lenape.

And never for the rest of my life did I ever get it right.

Purgatory Hill

"Hoc est Corpus meum."
"This is my body."

—Robert Curly, Age 13

It wasn't like I never saw him.

Maybe it would be monthly. Or I would see him briefly with his parents, going somewhere he didn't want to go, or looking out of his bedroom window reflected behind a tangle of tree limbs. At thirteen, he stopped going to regular school, and stopped playing ball with us in the street. Most of all, he stopped being an altar boy.

I was prone to mysteries and enigmas—the Bermuda Triangle, dark matter, pi—but nothing was more pregnant in my imagination than the riddle of Bobby Curly. The more they hid him, the more I thought I saw him.

It wasn't like we were best friends or anything. I don't think Bobby Curly ever had a best friend—on this earth. A few years later though, he became mine.

The guys made up stories. He was caught robbing a bank, or he was between acts of a sex change. It was suggested he was involved with something unthinkably noble, like donating a kidney to save a stranger's life, or the Blessed Virgin appeared to him in Prospect Park like Saint Bernadette at Lourdes.

Whatever it was, we knew it was something Big. Something Romantic or Horrible, but Big. And it was a long, bleak passage through some branch of unhappiness and shame before Bobby Curly came back to us in the summer of 1965.

It took a half-dozen trips to Purgatory Hill when we were sixteen with a six-pack of beer for me to get it out of him. Even then—although Bobby was presumably at the center of his own disappearance—it was like he was figuring it out for the first time. None of us bothered him about his secrets since he came back to us a few months earlier, although it would be a coup for me to find out.

Purgatory Hill was ten blocks away, on the edge of a fancy-ass country day school, the only one of its kind in the city. To us, its magnificence was real, but uncalled for. The local kids, when we dared, clambered up the hill for easy access to the school from Seventh Avenue to make forays into the delights of the grounds, which included lakes, fruit trees, rolling hills, grass lawns, and rich, preppy schoolboys to fuck with.

The school was fenced on all sides; a barrier between the heaven of the campus grounds and the Saint Anne architecture of the academic buildings versus the perdition of Seventh Avenue, and the crowded streets and apartments where we lived. The official entrance to the grounds was a high, black gate with spearheads like a medieval castle, the rest low hurricane fencing to keep out riffraff dogs and the local kids.

Bobby and I sat on Purgatory Hill one summer afternoon with a can of beer between our legs overlooking the school's four-sided clock tower, one of the urban wonders of the world, rising into the sky in the middle of Brooklyn.

Two human-made lakes provided mirrors for apple trees and lanes for affluent schoolboys to stride with book bags, in prep school indifference, toward becoming grown-up tax attorneys and proctologists. A second wave of schoolboys were getting out of club meetings and afternoon team practices, heading for the buses. If they saw just the two of us, they might take a quick foray up the hill in slope-shouldered hostility to check us out.

A few years prior, a squad of upperclassmen charged in a coordinated assault up the hill against our sideways football game in the snow. First, we sent down dogs and the younger kids barking and shouting into their forward ranks. The rest of us fell into them like blue tattooed Picts between their ears with our fists and heads, sending them bleeding down the hill with torn school jackets and hats blowing in the wind back to the yellow buses.

On top of the hill, two yards behind Bobby and me was a sharply angled dirt cliff with exposed tree roots, where rain rushed down ruts and onto our side of Seventh Avenue. Abandoned lots and houses predominated for blocks. There wouldn't be any cars if not for a half-dozen wrecks where bums slept, and guys said they got blowjobs.

Everywhere, bags of fast food, beer cans and whiskey bottles, dirty magazines, and scummy old condoms—by volume, in that order—landscaped the street like the grasses and tumbleweeds of the empty western plains.

We sat on what grass there was. I tried to jump-start him with details about things the guys speculated about his separation: psychological personnel seemed involved, or religious counselors; home schooling was surely in effect. Priests in three-piece black priest-suits from outside the parish passed through the Curly apartment spreading hopes among the gang of exorcisms.

Halfway into his second beer, Bobby glanced at an angle into the lowering sun like he had a bit-part in a B-movie, and said, "I missed a lot of good times, didn't I, Richie?"

"Not really."

I couldn't lie to him. At least he was making progress. He still hadn't looked at me, but instead trained a distanced unfocus on the school's clock tower to position the shifts and movement of the sky flying behind it—and perhaps memories cast in retrospect.

He said, "It was my Grannie the first time." Now we were

getting somewhere, but this didn't sound so good. Clouds continued to fly behind the tower with rumors of the Atlantic rasping five blocks behind the Veterans Hospital. It was kind of pleasant.

Bobby added, "She was house-ridden."

I didn't push him. We continued looking at the big clock on the side of the tower we could see from the hilltop as if that was our only option, considering the drawn-out nature of what Bobby was saying. We estimated it was four-thirtyish.

The neighborhood gang blew the clock's eight-foot minute hand off a few years before with an explosive made of cherry bombs, tape, and roman candles. People could see it as far away as Bensonhurst. There were unspoken teenage medals for bravery awarded, and legends bestowed that night that could make or destroy a boy's future. I held a ladder.

Ten minutes later, as if part of one stretched-out thought, he said, "She lived from the big living-room chair next to the piss-bucket, to the bed. Mom or Sis washed her with a face cloth every day. Real quick, like she was a Chevy or something."

But it was after we slid down the cliff back of Purgatory Hill to the macadam barrens of the neighborhood to walk off the beers that Bobby had anything interesting to say.

"I told her not to tell anybody."

Our sense of time was speeding or the fabric of space shrinking. Or space was expanding as time slowed. Either way, we were in no condition to make the call.

Nevertheless, the effect of the beer on him on the way home was: he told me one Sunday during Mass he slipped several consecrated hosts under his white altar boy cassock after serving communion with Father Smith before the tabernacle lock-up of the leftovers. These were activated, "live hosts," Bobby said, "their essences transubstantiated into the

Body of Jesus Christ like tiny hand grenades with their pins pulled, ready to go off. For the flesh of God to fly like shrapnel into the souls of communicants waiting with their eyes closed and tongues hanging out."

An excess of alcohol made him sound like that.

He proceeded to tell me, later that night, he held a host before his Grannie's face, simmering with God's grace—the face that wept when he broke his arm and beamed when he got his first Little League hit.

He held it between his index finger and thumb to deliver the light of everlasting life.

"Hoc est corpus meum."

He knew the words and had the moves. He improvised with personal flourishes and under-the-circumstances economies. And poor Mrs. O'Boyle let the Body of Jesus Christ be placed on her tongue by her beloved grandson and melt into her soul as in a dream.

And she told no one.

We went weekly to Purgatory Hill throughout the summer while Bobby wrestled to recover lost memories. Sometimes he remembered nothing. Other times, there would be stirrings of new recollections studded with glimmers of the Power, and there would be glimpses of the Glory.

I began to see why Bobby Curly had to go away from us for a while.

As the earth slanted into grayest November, we returned to Purgatory Hill between Bandit Avenue and Paradise Prep, hopefully for the last time. I suggested adding a joint I acquired to our usual six-pack we carried up the cliff-face. A school security truck stopped on the road at the base of the hill.

The security personnel were alert to the neighborhood boys. Our extermination or effective containment was prominent in their job descriptions. We were juvenile coyotes pawing at the borders of the squire's animal preserve.

"Get the hell out'a here before I come up there, ya punks. Move!" He gunned his truck halfway up the hill.

We opened our first beers. If we stayed to the hilltop, our exit down the cliff and over the fence onto Seventh Avenue was likely.

"You were saying about your grandmother."

It was the first time I pushed him.

"What did I say?"

"Nothing. You copped a couple'a hosts and gave one to your granny."

"I know."

An apple tree trembled near the clock tower moments before a few hundred of the year's last starlings emerged squawking on the branches and twigs, delirious for migration.

The young birds beat shining, newly preened feathers like flying Zulu warriors for their first flight, while the old bore rumpled, molting heads for their last to the eating grounds and chirping fields of the southern meadows. All waited for one overwrought bird to make the breakout move.

"I went from that, to pretty much everything else in a quick couple'a weeks."

The sky was blank. One jumpy bird could stand it no longer, and, with one high-octave whistle, they exploded into a raucous cheer and were off. Bobby wondered if any birds were left behind. We thought what that might be like—to be a disabled, old, or forgotten bird in an empty tree.

The beer made everything skittery to understand where we were, or what we were doing—but the addition of the weed and the birds made it seem like a new order was falling on us, which took a long course of concentration to master.

Then he remembered how he got to be "doing the priest," as he put it. To be set apart. I tried to imagine. To be an interpreter of the faithful—of the strange ways of God and the Church.

We thought about it while looking for clouds and watching birds fill the sky to the south, heading for the high-rise projects of Coney Island.

There were two beers left, and the joint's slow decline made us appear profound as the afternoon left the sky. Bobby's normal restraint was turning hazy in the twilight.

"Grannie didn't care how authentic the host was, but that was everything to me, so I always tried to get a consecrated host or two and said the words exact, like Smith or Father Lynch. I was doing all Jesus or nothing. I knew the Latin, so I staged it to line up with their forgot memories."

"Their?"

"Besides my Granny was my aunt's mother-in-law, Mrs. Apple—totally outside her skull down the hall. Sometimes, I gathered them together like sheep. They were so pale from being inside you could almost see through them."

"Jesus, Bobby."

"It wasn't like they seriously counted them. It began to feel like I was on the dusty road with Jesus to the Last Supper. And me, a little shit kid, with the old ladies looking at me like I'm some kind'a angel. I could of served them bits of hotdog buns for all they knew. You know what it's like to feel that at thirteen? An angel, Richie, or some brand of saint? Do you?"

I did not.

"I would have served goblets of Sacred Blood if I could cop the wine," he said.

"There were confessions, too, with not a real sin between them. More like missed opportunities. Like, 'I should have been stricter with your mother.' Things like that. It had to end badly."

The air held hints of winter when the wind blew, and the shadows took the tone of the sun's dying glow. Still no clouds. Just then our mothers would be boiling water for dinner while we were out of our minds sitting like tiny specks on the darkening hill.

We stabbed open our last beers, which spewed into our faces. The prevailing thought was, we might as well deaden ourselves to what we were about to face from our mothers for missing dinner, with our fathers probably searching for us. But we were too dug in—with Bobby spilling his guts at an unprecedented rate—to change course.

"I knew I made them feel holy, at least. There were home visits for 'the infirmed' by the parish, but nothing like me. I drew out each minute."

"It's not like you were freakin' evil, Bobby. You were doing tons of good, right? Not like you was robbing banks or whacking off or nothing."

"No, Richie. It was worse. I was tugging at the curtain behind where the Wizard played with the whistles and the secret gears that don't really do shit, and I was playing along as if I was part of it. Father Lynch turns bread into God and wine into the Savior's blood who died for our sins. That's as high as a man gets, if anyone believes you. While I was a thirteen-year-old playing priest with hosts I stole for two senile old women. I had to be defrocked. As a human being."

He looked into the empty sky.

He got caught when his mother found her son with the ecclesiastical goods and went to Father Lynch for advice. Bobby had been Saint Robert Curly for exactly three months. Because of his youth, his case was considered redeemable and taken extremely seriously by Church authorities. There were also fears of the appearance of the stigmata, unprecedented at such a young age, which threatened. Interventions were initiated—on earth as in heaven.

Traffic picked up along the avenue as guys gunned hot rods to beat the light on Eighty-Sixth Street. I could barely follow what Bobby was saying in the decline of the beer and the joint almost gone between us on the border of Brooklyn and Fairyland. I could hear him talking and I remembered what he said in a once-removed way, like the details of certain dreams stay with a person throughout their lifetime.

We sat on our skinny, bony asses, doing nothing—like boozy chimpanzees making pale shadows onto the avenue in the setting sun. In the sky behind the school's clock tower, an enormous meteor—or fireball—the relative circumference on the horizon of a large star, sparkled toward us from the west at approximately 45,000 miles per hour, set at a negative two-degree angle to the surface of the earth. Somewhere over Ohio or Pennsylvania, and moving fast, it was on a journey begun three and a quarter billion years earlier. It kept coming until it was the size of the searing white headlight of a locomotive, tracking toward the school's clock tower and Purgatory Hill.

What I saw and what the Fireball implied—whether the Eye of God or the iron cast of a dumb stone—I tried over the years to understand. Bobby Curly also saw what he saw in the mazy early evening. He seemed oddly ready for it.

The hill quaked. Our downy little hairs ionized. The estimated mass of the Fireball when it reached Purgatory Hill was about eight spinning school buses. We knew the thing was neither friend nor foe. Nor did it notice us when it passed over our heads into the flatlands of Brooklyn, where it likely exploded or sparked away like a punk snuffed out between two fingers.

Our attention soon braced back to the clock tower in anticipation of being swept by the terrible after-wind. Instead, we were met with a gentle breeze as Purgatory Hill dropped back into the Om of the universe.

We said nothing as we slid down the dirt cliff of Purgatory Hill into the dark, empty streets. I did not recall walking home. I told my father I was sorry, but not for what. I was filthy and didn't care what he did to me. I don't think he did anything. Mom brought food to my room which I didn't touch.

The next day, there was no word of fireballs. Not at school, nor in the local papers. We knew what we knew, even if there were no words for it.

We went to Purgatory Hill more regularly, but different people. We sat stacked back-to-back on the hill, matter-of-fact sober. An amped-up recording of "Taps" played—as it always played—at five p.m. from nearby Ft. Hamilton to remind the neighbors of the long desolation of death. We sat.

"Richie? What does God look like? How 'bout non-God? What does It look like?"

I shrugged against his shoulders.

"Maybe you'll find out one day. Probably not," he said.

As Brooklyn receded into winter, we went to Purgatory Hill until the first snow-cover in case it came back. It did not.

The Fireball's effect obliterated rote liturgies, mythologies, priests and mullahs, gurus, lords and masters, police officers, parents, faeries. I wasn't that animistic to begin with, but it would be nice to understand what and if there was meaning behind fireballs, God, and the cosmos. Even senseless stones from the beginning of time. If you include beer and weed in the mix, I had a lot of questions.

Not, however, Bobby Curly. The meaning of life simply flipped. Click!

Bobby stopped being sorry for how he behaved at thirteen when for a few months he stole hosts and performed magic to anesthetize loved ones into believing they were going to heaven —or were already there—and did things to make himself a bit like the priests he admired—and his hero, Jesus.

Weirdly capricious and tricky-looking girls loved him, and he loved them. He appreciated on-the-edge creations in any form and loosely embraced metaphysical theories without much attention to what they implied, provided they promised hidden beauty or strange surprise. Allen Ginsberg. Wilhelm Reich. The Velvet Underground. Warhol!

At eighteen, he got his draft card and burned it. Later, he refused to serve when compelled.

Meanwhile, he joined and organized sit-ins and protests, fasts-for-peace, teach-ins, and teach-outs. He made a small-time name for himself. Me? I went off, deferred from the Vietnam War, to study liberal arts at the City College of New York. Bobby got himself arrested. He rejected legal defenses and laughed at jail time.

"I wasn't aware Brooklyn declared war on anybody," he said.

It was an interesting, if legally unimpressive defense—but the Brooklyn press ate it up. Even as the war wound down, Bobby faced five years in prison.

After months of legal squabbles, prosecution became a pain for the authorities, and the case was dismissed.

When a feature appeared in The Bay Ridge Spectator with a picture of him staring into the camera lens holding a live butterfly in his palm, he got a scholarship from an anonymous benefactor to the Department of Religious Studies at New York University, where he crafted a lonely and useless degree in Ancient Middle Eastern Creeds and Beliefs.

He understood more about Gnostic, Coptic, Manichaean, Zoroastrian, and early Christian rituals, rebel gospels, and agape lovefests than any living soul in New York cared to.

A year after he graduated, Bobby's hybrid memoir of his life thus far, JESUS and THE FIREBALL, came out.

A rambling free-verse composition inside a Trout Fishing in America-style travelog, roughly about his altar boy days and subsequent adventures, it recommended a confusing "know what you know then forget about it" philosophy. Printed by a third-rate press, it wasn't meant to make money, and didn't. But it found a common thread among the rad college crowd and hippie religionists.

A few downtown bookstores sold it for near nothing as a local oddity. The various Brooklyn churches, synagogues, and mosques joined together in ecumenical hatred to keep it out of the larger book outlets. It received what circulation it got by being left on subways and in student common areas.

While he unofficially disappeared into the paved apartment-building hills and valleys of Brooklyn, I discovered him—or thought I did, as was my custom, where I least expected—in lots and under bridges with people around flaming barrels, and heard his voice on the radio on the high channels late at night reading poems I did not understand. I would find him smiling at me coming out of side streets and old men's after-hours bars at dawn while I was going to work.

I had no idea where he lived. One morning, while driving in rush hour traffic on the Gowanus Expressway to an interview in the city for a job I didn't want, I sighted him near the ill-defined edges of a junkyard near a shanty in Red Hook, on a street with no name.

It took a half-hour to drive into and out of dead ends and fetid inlets with broken ferries and warehouses under circling gulls, before… There he was, leaning against a giant rain barrel.

"I saw you sightseeing around the neighborhood, you eejit. I hope you're staying."

He was happy to show me around, but neither the purpose nor function of the place made sense. It made scant money while free exchanges of abandoned objects happened. There was no landlord, no address. Apparently, there were spontaneous gatherings, singsongs for passersby, and scrap collages were made, for no apparent reason, into towers teetering into the junkyard sky.

He said, "Pretty soon, freeform churches sprouted and staked out sites for spontaneous rituals and community love-making. I have nothing to do with them. Unless they ask."

He seemed in charge, but his influence was in a squatter's-rights sense—being in negative possession of the place. I was hopelessly late for my interview, so I took his invitation to spend the night.

Seven bridges crossed the Gowanus Canal, the most polluted body of water in the Americas, north or south. Seemingly incompatible with plant or animal life, its chemical waters regularly caught fire, "which consumed some of the more poisonous gases," he said. "Once a cat made it to the other side on top of the vapors before it fell dead. Where else could you live and die for free and do what you have to?"

I stayed that night and all day Saturday. Bobby was the same as I remembered, yet different—the way people show new aspects and add access without changing.

As we continued his junkyard tour, the wasteland before us seemed to become more purposed. He said people came to explore, dump unwanted machinery and furniture, or take home what they wanted.

While I was there, sofas, stoves, bongs, dogs, cats, and birds in cages—once an infant in a basket—were left by people who couldn't care for them and taken home by people who would.

Also on the property was a bulletin arrangement where secrets and wishes along with notices, declarations of independence, codices, stelae, Magna Cartas, or unpublishable stories and poems were pinned. More like a 35-foot clothesline strung between metal poles with a twist in the middle to provide a flip each time around the circuit. Bobby said it was technically a Möbius strip, but people called it "The Direct Line," where people mostly clipped the awful things they wanted to apologize to the world for, or to ask forgiveness from a person they couldn't face. A person might also take credit for something wonderful that went unnoticed.

"Like a soapbox for silent brags or a confessional for abominations," Bobby said. "Without priests or lawyers—it's an improvement. It's also free."

Monthly, The Direct Line was cleared, and the notes burned while people watched or not.

"One guy apologized for slavery," Bobby said. "His confession wrung around The Line 360 degrees for three weeks. He felt personally responsible. Maybe he was. Still, it was a nice thing to do."

"Ever put anything on The Line yourself?" I asked.

"Once."

He wasn't about to tell me, was he? When a young couple

came to The Line, he said, "Come on, let's take a walk." So we did.

In front of an assortment of concrete birdbaths he stopped to ask me, "Ever wonder if what happened on Purgatory Hill really happened?"

"What's the difference whether something happened or we thought it happened?" I asked.

"It would be all the same to us, right?"

"I took credit and apologized for The Fireball," he admitted. "I wrote a book about it, remember? I just wanted it go away."

"I wish I had a Direct Line."

"You do."

Cops surveilled from cars parked under the elevated highway while drinking coffee or reading papers. The department conducted regular raids for contraband and enforced subpoenas regarding officious regulations leading to vengeful judgments. Bobby refused to pay kickbacks, graft, or fines whether he had the money or not.

"If I was profiting from some scheme, I would fit in the system. Give a little, take a little. I wasn't playing, so I was fined for things I didn't do or couldn't pay for. I was locked up a lot. I admit some of what went on here wasn't always up to community standards, but it's the 1970s for frig sakes. You'd think they would like to know what's going on. Wouldn't you?"

When it was dark, we hopped over a brass walrus and around a carving of a large wooden baseball glove at the entrance of a plywood and tin building supported by concrete blocks—home to everyone there, known and unknown.

Under an Aster Place street sign, the influence of cheap wine, and smoke from an unusual plant, he explained the details of his current project: The People's Streets. "Streets" was a confederacy of raiders who ripped down street signs named after crooked NYC politicians, power brokers, and robber barons ever since New York was New Amsterdam.

"We put up signs to honor ordinary people who did nice things for their neighbors: tutored kids, cleaned lots, fostered children—or provided a room to a family in need. That sort'a thing."

A half-mile stretch of Vanderbilt Avenue was stripped of signs and replaced in the safety of night with "People's Street Signs"—Mrs. Fernandez Place, Mama Paula Street, Frank Avenue, Pizza Man Court, and Coach Tyrell Road. Horns honked and neighbors ate, drank, and danced at ad hoc festivals for weeping honorees. In a few days the Department of Transportation had the old ones remade and reinstalled.

"They never could pin anything on us. They just figured it was connected to the Junk Yard in some way."

Then the restraining orders, arrests, and fines for petty offenses would start.

"We didn't care. I doubt Carnegie ever had a street party for him, but Izzy Goldberg who ran a free food bank did. Sometimes, if we asked nice, the DOT workers would give us our signs back. It was something you'd remember forever on your kitchen wall."

He said to come back Tuesday night, late, if I want some action. "We're replacing two blocks of Nostrand Avenue. I don't know who Nostrand was, but we have great people living there who need street signs. Mr. Nostrand will be back in business before he knows it, which he doesn't."

He got my I'll-see shrug.

Way after midnight, Bobby helped me to an extra sleeping bag which I squeezed into across from a girl who looked into my eyes until I drifted off.

In the morning, we talked with our heads sticking out of our polyester cocoons at each other.

She was up early to prepare herself for tomorrow's events.

"Although there's nothing really to prepare for except practice loosening up my center of gravity for what's coming. It's not that easy, really." Her name was Barbara. I expected Misty Blue or Moon Bacon.

"I'll sneak from place to place, maybe listen, sing along if I feel it. It's like a crazy circus. There would be elephants and serpents if they had any. Maybe tomorrow. I visit if there seems to be a portal to somewhere inviting. Sometimes I dance with who's there. Alchemic altogether."

She was neither pretty nor unpretty, as if her looks didn't matter to her and so shouldn't to me—and that's how I looked at her.

"The Sunday Encounters are so extra ordinary, so innermost. Just completely hoodwinking—in a sort of corporeal, under-religious way. I keep getting drawn back to figure what's going on. Irreal! You know? Like it's a different amniotic emergence every time, entirely."

This speech was delivered in the interrogatory mood with the help of her eyes and body leans. I made nods and affirming noises, even though I could only guess what she meant.

"Do you always talk like that?"

"No. Almost."

We decided to walk around the industrial shoreline to look at the wrecks and debris.

The waterfront was edged by a wooden seawall seasoned by salty water, wind, seabird guano, and the sun. Later, we figured Bobby set us up for some reason, which would be like him, although he never said.

Floating in the water were barges, remnants of docks, and hundreds of bobbing bottles, paper bags, and barrels. All, great and small, rose together in the tide, serenaded by the moaning of wood against metal and metal against wood.

In front of us, a broken, rusting ferry rose and fell in harmony with a soup can.

"You want to develop a theory for it?" I asked.

"Totally."

I grabbed her hand and inched her to where our legs dangled over the oily water to articulate "the ferry and the can phenomenon."

I remembered a Galileo experiment with a cannonball and a feather dropped together from a tower landing simultaneously. Perhaps it was an egg. I admitted I likely got it wrong, and I knew it had nothing to do with buoyancy.

"It probably was Leonardo, anyhow." I said.

Barbara thought it was possible for bonding to be achieved between inanimate objects in any medium, if onlookers were in tune with the objects and each other, in time together with everything else.

"The simultaneity of unlikely things," she called it.

"Like a pointillist flower is more than specks on a canvas if you're looking at it with the right influx of meaning. Like a togetherness collage in a touching embrace."

She blamed Einstein and Seurat "for any confusions."

"Do you always talk that way?"

"No. Never."

After a straw poll, I kissed her when she won two to none.

We made coffee in Bobby's hut and walked through parts of the junkyard she wanted to see. I told her I let her win our contest and I didn't believe her theory, but I admitted, "You're a terrific kisser."

"Well, you're an okay kisser yourself, but I didn't believe my idea either. I just wanted to see how gullible you were."

We walked through unwanted appliances and furniture from the surrounding world and tried to find philosophies for them, but settled instead for building a junk tower. We piled things like sofas and stoves together for the base, then added lighter stuff like chairs and tables up to a rooster weathervane on top that pointed its beak away from the wind.

"Do you believe people on the expressway will see it?" she asked.

"Probably not, heh?" She was right.

When we finished our pointless junk-tower, we walked around, checking out piles of this and heaps of that.

Typewriters. Bird feeders. Feltless pool tables. I decided to stay another day.

At dawn, "services" from eclectic eras and traditions throbbed through Red Hook and Cobble Hill before being drowned out by expressway traffic. Sabian, Hebrew, and Christian remembrances, Muslim songs in Arabic, and Wicca/Celtic hybrids began in corners and out-buildings. Secret rites and holy orgasms happened in secret places, people spun in circles, and moans moaned in the shallows while cops drank coffee in their cars.

It was entertaining, but by noon, I had seen and heard a lifetime's worth. For the first time, I considered seriously shedding the rude joys of youth for steady work in the civil service, with a uniform and a badge like the cops napping under the highway or firemen like my uncles. The Transit Authority held promise. There was this girl down the block I liked okay.

Bobby Curly and I said goodbye near what may have been the junkyard's entrance, next to a painted sign with a quote from St. Thomas's Gospel:

"'Be Passersby.' – Jesus."

An odd convergence of time with no future tense passed as we looked at each other and I knew we would always find each other. I offered to buy the brass walrus and wooden glove.

"They're yours. Take them."

I had nowhere to put them nor did I know why I wanted them. We squeezed the walrus into my back seat. It made the hood ornament point a foot higher into the sky. The glove was not happening.

"Come on. Let me give you something."

"Na. It's yours. Don't forget to feed it. You can pick up the glove whenever."

Barbara was not to be found. Perhaps she found a place of grace. Bobby slipped me her number just in case.

When I got home, my mother said a woman named Barbara called. My father helped me walk the walrus up the stairs. He loved that I had at least one crazy friend left. I propped it sideways so its big head looked out my window.

Within a year of trying on the Transit Authority, I couldn't hack the rattling bedlam of the subways, nor the okay girl down the block. Barbara, my junkyard girl, was totally back in my life after a few months. She had her fill of her "junkyard services," too.

"Once 'priests and priestesses' happened, it was all about them," she said.

"Then the professional Buddhists and Maharishis got involved. Forget it."

We occasionally visited Bobby to make Junk Towers, even though they were practically invisible.

Something about senseless creative gestures excited us. Mostly, we had walking dates along Shore Road or went into the Village to see Warhol films and listen to music at the Café Wha? and Gerde's Folk City.

After a few months, Barbara and I moved upstate to Beacon, N.Y. on the Hudson River to run a dilapidated antique-and-everything-used store that we leased on the cheap, with an apartment upstairs. Artsy folks—mostly musicians and painters—had been invading the Hudson Valley since the mid-sixties—Dylan, The Band, Kerouac, Janis. It seemed a thing to do.

I bought an old pick-up to take the walrus with us to the country, snatching the giant baseball glove from Bobby along the way. I made him take twenty bucks.

I dragged the walrus outside the store daily to guard the entrance of our Everything Store and dragged it back every night. After a while, I left it out, even if it snowed. Who'd steal it? The Wooden Glove stayed inside to greet people like an open hand. Little kids sat and played in it while their parents shopped.

We gave away copies of Bobby's Jesus and The Fireball we displayed in the window. People took more if we changed the cover to Buddha and The Fireball although we didn't change the text. Nobody seemed to notice or didn't say. Bobby promised a long visit. He said he'd bring someone "if they could make love in the glove."

While city officials continued punishing Bobby for not

being corrupt, he noticed instead of turning on, tuning in, and dropping out, folks were coming to the Junk Yard seeking their identities. Knowing these items were unavailable for cash or barter, he gave the place away to a raggle-taggle collusion of whoever was there. He didn't own it anyway.

Bobby fled to a Fort Greene flat where he joined an occult music group to play the udu and sleep with people he liked. Sometimes he wrote poetry to keep his name in the world—four-dimensional poems no one was meant to understand. He promised us a poem about Zeno and Saint Thomas we could hang in our store's window. We doubted we would understand it.

"If I understood it, you think I could write it?"

In the middle of the night a few months later, Robert Curly Boulevard signs went up across the city from Staten Island to the Bronx and out onto the Island. They were hammered out on tin and wooden placards and repurposed license plates. When the Department of Transportation took one down, two went up.

Bobby had been murdered in a holding cell in police custody, charged with criminal trespass and destruction of city property in the act of liberating a howl of condemned shelter dogs into the streets. He was big on imprisoned animals and canine murder. No one was ever charged with his killing. "Happens all the time," we were told by a cop friend. "It was bound to happen someday. A mob hit or an accident on purpose as a favor for a city official who didn't ask for it. Jail ain't safe. 'Specially if you're Bobby Curly, who's a pain in the ass."

Eventually, two signs were let remain by the DOT over the

Red Hook junkyard on the corner of Robert Curly Boulevard and Shelter Dog Avenue.

On the day I found out about Bobby, while walking with Barbara along a Beacon street, I spotted a fireball in the afternoon sky like eight spinning fiery school buses. I had been expecting it. I pointed it out to several people as it passed overhead. They looked up, but either didn't see it, or weren't interested.

I found it strange how some things—like fireballs—once you saw one, while you never had to see another, you always did. And if you never had, you probably never would.

Barbara grabbed my arm and put her head on my shoulder. I told her all I knew about fireballs: how big, how fast, how old, where from, and whether there was a cosmology behind them. She held me tighter. She was the kind of girl I could say things like that to—as long as I really didn't know.

"Would you explain it again later?" she asked. "Please? I'd like that."

"Want to find a philosophy for it?"

"Yeah. That would be good. I'll win though."

"I'm looking forward."

"I'm epitomizing ideas already."

She said, "You know those priests and counselors they sent to work over Bobby when he was an altar boy? I think they were worried he was getting into Holy Ghost territory. Ever see a painting of the Holy Ghost that isn't some bird or beam of light?"

She squeezed tighter. "Or maybe," she said. "He was leaving the Trinity behind for some brand of doggishness altogether."

In the vastness of the cosmos, how quaint we must have appeared walking home under the Beacon sky. Me seeing flaming asteroids and her inventing theories for Bobby being

Bobby. We sat in front of the fireplace that night while the wood collapsed.

A week later, we traveled to Brooklyn to visit family and friends and see the street signs over Bobby's junkyard. While we were there, his ashes were scattered over Purgatory Hill.

Only a handful paid their respects, most of whom I didn't know, including a pair of off-duty cops I could tell by the way they moved around each other. Maybe they were on duty. We all climbed the dirt cliff off Seventh Avenue on my suggestion, even though we probably could have walked through the entrance.

We spread Bobby's ashes and said what we were thinking or moved our mouths. One man shook his head. "Nobody gets killed in police custody by mistake," he said like he knew. "Not over dogs."

As darkness overtook the neighborhood, streetlights lit up, headlights turned on, and switches flipped in homes and apartment buildings. It made the sea fog seem thicker. Bobby's farewell party walked down the hill to the road and out the front gate. Barbara and I slid down the cliff to Seventh Avenue in honor of Bobby. A very bad idea. Perfect for us.

We drove by Bobby's old junkyard on a whim of mine on the way to the tunnel into the city. I took a minute alone under Bobby's street sign. We agreed to drive to Beacon the long way along the Taconic Parkway.

Turning into Manhattan, the lights of the skyscrapers broke up on the river on its way to the ocean. We headed north into pale cliffs and hills, and the lights of river towns like Sleepy Hollow, Ossining, and Stony Point shined in the dark as I concentrated on the road while she rested her hand on my leg and looked toward the west, in case the river should reappear through the trees and foothills, giving me extra eyes to imagine what she saw.

She was talkative. It was right to have her. She was on about moving back to Brooklyn—for a million reasons. All of which I understood, like we didn't really need another excuse for not raising a family "away from the clamoring crickets."

I promised to find a way out of our lease and maybe scout the Board of Ed for substitute teacher jobs.

It was always cold enough for a small fire, which I made while Barbara readied for bed. I went outside to the back of the truck to retrieve the Robert Curly Boulevard sign I had stolen.

I sat on the tailgate. The night got colder, and the stars got sharper, and I could never cry when I had to. And when Barbara came out to wrap me next to her in her winter coat to take me inside, I could; and when I did, I couldn't stop until we got around the fire to find a philosophy for it. Which we did. She did.

"It's a laurel, Richie, or a street sign. Or a boundary herald to announce the coming and leaving of Bobby Curly's life, for his love and despair for himself and us, the dogs, and space rocks unexplainable in the cosmos and the way the junkyard used to be. For everything that changes and is the same. For a while, a storm blew through our world and you're holding what's left."

"Do you always talk that way?"

"Not yet."

Snakes in The Garden

> "Killing a snake is the same
> as having a snake."
>
> —Joan Didion

Bay Ridge, Brooklyn, NY
[Winter, 1972]

A large clay and plaster likeness of Saint Patrick, holding a crook and pointing at snakes frozen in time on the statue's base, was wheeled in face up on a donkey cart as if in a funeral procession. It was winched upright into place by strong men when Saint Patrick's Church on Ninety-Fifth Street in Brooklyn, New York, was built. It was the worst of the famine years back home. "Black '47," my father called it.

Patrick gazed over our heads from his pedestal at the front right of the church ever since.

Once installed, he never once moved. But the right appetite in the right person, paired with perfect atmospheric conditions, might move those eyes to look into your eyes. Perhaps a toke across the near-infrared window at the border of human perception or into the ultraviolet extent of the soul. It had been known to happen. Once, twice, a hundred times. If only for a twinkling, a Holy Saint might enter your inner self through the magic of each other's eyes.

I was beginning my thirteenth year in good standing with God and His Church. Tom Jones had won the Academy Award. The Gulf of Tonkin Resolution provided a credible deception for U.S. entry into the Vietnam War. Three civil rights workers were murdered in Mississippi. In Rome, Pope John XXIII passed away, with vision and affection, a few months earlier.

I did not expect the road to apostasy to be lit so brightly.

From an early age, I could sum up religion as one titanic struggle. The forces of Hell, Satan, Assistant Devils, Snakes, Sin, and Death were arrayed against Heaven, the Church Militant, the Churches Suffering and Triumphant, Jesus, God the Father, and the Dove; the Holy Spirit, all of the saints, and the Virgin Mary. You wouldn't think it would turn out to be much of a battle, considering the resources available and the advantage of having the Word on your side. But believe me, it was.

The outpatient facility where the spiritual battle casualties on the side of Good went for surgical repair was Holy Confession, which commenced from noon to five p.m. Saturdays since antiquity, regardless of how the civil world turned.

It was late autumn, when the sun was most bright and the clouds most dark. Rolling cascades of light were created when the sun, emerging from behind a speeding storm cloud, terraced the pews quicksilver one after another. Then everything flashed back into black shadow as a new cloud eclipsed the sun. Joseph, Patrick, and other celebrity saints looked ready to leap from their pedestals, dancers caught between strobes—the paint and plaster of our faith. But not Mary, Our Lady of Sorrows.

Mary looked down, the weeping soul and simple heart of the tempestuous, elliptical Godhead. Her arms and hands arched. Beneath her feet a serpent with an apple in its mouth writhed. It was unclear whether it was being constrained from attack or trying to escape. Nightly, snakes carpeted the floors of my dreams.

When the next in line entered Father Smith's confessional, the rest of us in the pews swung over our hands or hopped sideways a moment or two behind the previous penitent to assume the open spot, like a very large, sluggish caterpillar moved in rolling sections, or the wave at a ballgame.

An hour into the afternoon, with the full electromagnetic spectrum piercing the church, Father Lynch sat alone in his confessional booth. After a short minute of reflection, he opened the door to discover the wave rolling across the pews to be absolved by Father Smith. Lynch walked down the aisle toward us, working his tongue against his teeth.

"This pew, come with me."

I was the last kid in the pew of people ushered away toward Lynch's empty confessional like cattle mooing into the executioner's butcher stall. Because I was last out, I was first in—with only a moment to refine my guilty plea.

We were inclined to squeeze between the poles of truth and falsehood in halves and almosts, but it was impossible to fudge past Lynch. I got the lowdown on Father Lynch from my dad.

One Saturday, he puts on his hat and announces to the family at the kitchen table that he is off to Saint Pat's to confession.

I'm off to the park to play roller hockey when I see the man, my own father, sitting on a park bench feeding the pigeons and reading The Daily News backwards through the sports section. I'm on skates, so he hears me grinding across the concrete pathway before I'm halfway. He continues doing what he's doing until I'm standing in front of him. He is surprised to see me.

"Son? What about yourself?" he says.

"Dad, I thought you...?"

He says, "I'm confessin' to the birds, in a manner of speaking, as you plainly see." Not a twinkle.

No giving me the hooded eye with the sideways head. He's matter of fact about it, maybe slightly beatific. He goes on to explain the religious significance of what he is doing—that he has moved up in sanctitude to the point where he can communicate his intentions and sins to the pigeons, who are, despite their reputation, among the select species of "blessed creatures," he calls them, the moral equivalent of the Elephant or the Lamb.

"Besides, Mickey, I'm cutting down on me church time," he says.

"Did you ever see a place where more snakes slithered about?"

He is serious. He is my father, so I give him full benefit of the doubt, but I reckon he has his pigeons and his doves reversed.

What followed, oblique as it was, was as close to a direct passing down of wisdom as I ever got from him.

"Animals are the purest form concocted by Himself. No fussing around about them, tryin' out being this or that. They're as is to begin with," he tells me. I'm thinking what I could possibly say in reply.

"Total absent of sin," he goes on.

"Which is the plague of humankind since Adam and Eve got throwed out the Garden. Themselves, the animals and the birds, are incapable of it. Have you not seen Baby Jesus with the little bird on His finger like he's talking to the flying prophet of truth itself?"

He waves his hand as he speaks and the birds juke into the air before settling back to pluck among the peanut shells which are there.

"But Dad..."

The pause seems endless. Each of us searches for words to end it.

"Do you know what I am going to tell you?" he says. I'm leaning on my hockey stick.

He says, "Confession is perhaps the wrong way to characterize it. More like dealing with God's representatives—in a more relaxed exchange."

He rolls up his newspaper to point out the various collections of birds and prominent individuals.

"The priests in Saint Pat's are all here, in their purer, holier forms. In a higher condition of spirit, their methods more natural, having come closer to the original act of creation—as the Bible says. The birds of the air coming in Day Three, whereas the first man and woman don't arrive 'til Day Six."

It's ridiculous, of course. I doubt he has the days right. But I half believe he's serious. He was capable of great assertions. When I was a child, he confided how our family "back home" were intimate with the Pookas of the rocks and shorelands for hundreds and thousands of years.

"Yer great uncle had a tail," he told me.

"There was Aunt Nuala's giant donkey ears no man would go near without a whip. Me own Da was half a bird himself. Don't tell yer little brother and sister I told you any of this. You know how they are."

It's a perfect day for a hockey game. It's cool and cloudy; trees along the walkways with their leaves half off are whistling to the wind. He tells me the Rangers lost the previous night, as massive tankers leave and enter New York Harbor unnoticed through the mouth of the Narrows. But he notices something he has to impart to me immediately.

"Ah," he says.

"There's the crux of Father Lynch himself. In the center of the rumpus." He points to a common gray and white street pigeon who is giving the other birds the business.

He says, "He's got his spies and stool pigeons reportin' to him. Nobody cares more about the poor critters of the flock than Lynch. He is your bird if yer in need of a heart-to-heart examination of yer soul—if you can put up with his clatter."

"But Dad, they're pigeons. They only care about pigeons."

"I can see that with my own eyes. I'm not deef," he says. He's getting maybe a bit pissy. I back off.

After a while he says, "Well, there's no denyin' that. There's a challenge confessin' to the birds, yes, but that's the beauty of it. Less blathering in Latin and Bless Me Fathering and fuss over which Commandment is which regards particular sins."

And he's proud of himself for thinking of it as he tucks himself into his overcoat against the start of a late-autumn snow flurry.

"You won't tell yer little sister and brother now about our wee talk, will you, Mickey? Knowin' how they are," he says again and returns to reading backwards toward the page concerning the horses at Belmont Park.

I know he is always playing me to think we are sharing deep, mysterious enigmas suited only to ourselves, so I tell him, "Sure, Dad."

Skating back to my hockey game, I look at him sitting on the bench as blue jays dive into the pigeon scrum. He is straining over his bifocals in an effort to keep me in sight. I give him the raised one-hand hockey stick salute, but he doesn't see me.

Needless to say, Father Lynch's confessional was not my Saturday destination of choice.

I did a hasty examination of conscience crossing the aisle into his confessional. I was guilty. We were all guilty. It was with us since inception and before that it was inherited from Adam and Eve—which seems to be an unfair but painful truth.

We crossed the portal as inherent sinners and left in the state of grace or with the stain on our souls of lying to a priest, which meant through the chain of command—lying to God. Yes, we were all guilty. And we were sorry. And we'll never again, until next month when we might look for a different confessor priest or find new ways to confound the matter through ambiguity of word or bilious blot of memory.

My sins were minimal. Infantile. An average priest behind the screen would have difficulty restraining a chuckle. Lynch slapped back the screen. His profiled, chiseled head, huge in the aperture, focused my attention. And since I was the first to face him of the cohort of souls who spurned his line for Smith's, he was prepared. He adjusted his face and nodded into the wall before him for me to begin.

"Bless me Father for I have sinned. I disobeyed my father, Father, four times."

I was a little nervous, so I got right into my first sin. Standard stuff. I would have confessed to it even if I didn't do it. I also missed my morning and evening prayers X many times, appropriate for the time interval. I cursed three times, only about hockey and baseball, never taking the Lord's name in vain. I confessed to two lies. That was it.

A sticky, glottal sound came from Lynch's tongue as it pulled away from his hard palate.

"Clugk. Yes, my son. Lied about what?"

I froze. After a few moments of silence, his head still parallel, he asked more questions. No priest in my life ever probed beyond what I told him. Lied to whom? I forgot. To what end? I didn't know. What were my intentions? Never again. I was about to pronounce the words to pull the curtain down on the whole performance—"For these and for all my sins I am truly sorry"—and force my penance and exit when he asked, "Is there anything else one wishes to confess today, my son?"

I heard a distinct italic cast to one word that implied I was holding back a critical matter of conscience. I had a moment leaning over the abyss that would change my trust in Jesus Christ here and above, and how I viewed myself, the world, and everything in it for a very long time. I jumped into the fire.

I told him about Rosie. How I felt was hard to explain. I was thirteen. I told him I wanted to share existence with her. I forget the exact, unfortunate words. I told him I desired to live in her hair, inside her chocolate eyes with the orange, radiating galaxies, and twine my legs together with hers.

I leaned back from the screen, stunned by what I had said. I knew I did something to be guilty of, but my desires were little more than daydreams. My own father would have pulled out a tale from his bag of characters. How the Great Lefty took a knee in the nuts for testing Missy Mulligan's virtue or how Bicycle Charlie lived with pirates for twenty years after being warped by love at my age. Good for a laugh, but I'd get the point.

Lynch's head rotated toward me behind the screen like a mechanical fortune teller as his next inquiry slotted into place. Clack.

"Did one have impure thoughts with regards to this girl, my son?"

I must have made a sound, because he spoke to me again.

"Did one, my son, touch her inappropriately, here or there, or in an impure manner?"

I would touch her here or there or anywhere she wanted if that were possible.

"No, Father."

But that was just the set up. He knew his demographic and he knew his boy, because next he asked, "Did one excite oneself in the, so-called, genital area, my son?"

I shook my head. I nodded. I said things I don't remember.

He boxed my easily tractable mind into corners, danced verbal jabs, hooks, and double-crosses. I would have confessed to murder for him to stop. Then I said it. I said it in a split instant, the way a person jumps for no reason off a bridge or into eternity down an elevator shaft.

"Once, Father, I touched myself watching her skip rope with her girlfriends across the street." In heaven, God lifted an enormous eyebrow.

"Where did one touch oneself?"

"Near my bedroom window, Father."

"No. No. Where on one's body did one touch oneself?"

I lapsed into a kind of aphasia that seized my ability to make words. I didn't have to, because he was now on about the Occasions of Sin which included newspaper ads for women's underwear, Elizabeth Taylor movies, and looking out my window.

I touched myself, yes. It made her more an angel than she already was. My eyes filled. She softened. I said her name into the window. "*Rosie*," I said. I shut my eyes.

"*Oh, Rosie.*"

"What is it don't you understand?"

I understood nothing. Luckily, he was off now on a hissing exegesis about what happened to boys who masturbated themselves into bent, malfunctioning penises. How each sperm was a potential child like the Baby Jesus. How the seeds of humanity by the trillions died in the mountains, plains, and valleys of our underwear or were flushed in tissues down toilet bowls. I was a spawning salmon squirting my seed into shallow, eggless shoals.

He said when I did my penance, I should do so at Our Lady's statue, under her arching arms. I should contemplate the serpent under her feet with the apple of temptation in its mouth.

I said something about never again and for these and for all my sins and left the confessional purged of all sinfulness and self-respect.

I held the curtain open for another Child of God to take my place. Most of the penitents Lynch had rounded up from Father Smith's line had snuck back down the aisle or scattered away home or to the surrounding bars.

Sunlight slanted through the reds and yellows and blues of the stained-glass windows in shafts of dust and sheets of photons.

The only sounds were the random squeal of a sneaker, the rifle shot of a falling knee rest, or a solitary cough rasping a throat. My standing in reality was disturbingly queer. My feet lifted and lowered as the marble floor moved under me, propelling me down the aisle where rows of statues passed with contingent faces frozen toward heaven. One referred his hands to an exposed red stucco heart.

To the left of the altar, scores of candles burned in red glass cups. Want a date? Your mom's sick? For ten or twenty-five cents you could borrow a flame with a wick. The new flame pulled away without diminishing the original, then fired another as bright as the first.

This was between you and Our Lady above the candles. The single flame, the pre-genital mother of all these flames, passed the light in this way since 1847. There was no scorecard of the effects of the coins and the eternal flame on the world, but a dime was enough to keep the flame alive.

I knelt before Mary, looked at her and the serpent under

her foot looking up with me into her eyes. I lit a candle. I said half of the rosary I owed Father Lynch.

Going out the front door, I tossed my rosary into the lawn surrounding the concrete statue of the Patron Saint and a gathering of free birds foraging in front of the church, where it sank into the ivy. The next time I'd tell him every detail. I'd tell him how it felt to be thirteen.

I tried to reconcile myself on the way home to my shame and fathomless ignorance.

I met Frank Colucci on Ninety-Fourth Street; a guy I played PAL baseball with. We discussed how confession made you feel when you did something was so horrible, but you told the priest—and he treated it like nothing he hadn't heard before.

Away you flew with a new soul exchanged for the bag of bones you had been dragging around the previous weeks, which seemed like a century. He had just confessed his thirteen-year-old abominations to Father Smith. Frankie was as aware as I about these matters, so I gave him the nutshell sense of my Lynch experience. He didn't respond except to nod.

We remembered Father Lynch from elementary school where he was called to explain why the sixth graders needed schooling in the proper habits and appearance of Catholic boys and girls, because Agnes Scaglione wore her hair one day in a ponytail revealing parts of her neck. Or why the seventh grade needed to comprehend the Virgin Mary was a virgin before and after giving birth to Jesus, and why that mattered. Why the teen dance at St. John's Lutheran Church, open to all teenagers, wasn't, according to Father Lynch, open to us.

Nothing happened to the families served by Saint Patrick's Parish, but Father Lynch poked into it for our own good.

Sitting on a park bench, Colucci and I determined life was too complex to worry about or try to understand, but that it was nearly impossible to ignore. We entered certain pacts regarding Father Lynch's future.

That day I was joined by a hardness. A self-critical, demi-self was introduced into me. Unlike a Guardian Angel or Patron Saint who would look after my interests, this flagellant Me both lashed and felt the pain.

It was Father Lynch who tipped me in this direction. In others, it was other priests or nuns, episcopal ministers of righteous temperaments, sudden fevers, or unaccountable nightmarish events.

Often it was superego manifestations brought on by oppressive parents, school, or work. I'm told Jewish children developed an inner presence that examined and reported back like mirrors reflecting off mirrors. Throw in pre-Iliad, Paleo people experiencing evolving bicameral chatter across the hemispheres of their perceived selves. Also: paranoids, poets, amnesiacs, and writers generally. Calvinists, too.

Over time, I learned to turn small, non-truths for effect—to play behind carefully constructed poses. I pretended to be smiling at some witty, internal thought, when it was an empty gesture meant to deceive a pensive high school girl on the subway. What was real but that which was perceived, and I perceived myself as I wanted others to see me.

I smoked cigarettes to encloud myself in mystery, for my face to emerge from behind the haze like Bogart in Casablanca or stuck small, phallic Clint Eastwood cigars between my teeth to jut like hood ornaments into the enemy world.

I began to wear certain clothes for effect, angled my cap and adjusted my collar, struck attitudes in raincoats against lampposts, even when no one was around. Because with the new me, there was always someone around. I worked for a month on a poem I passed off in English class as written in haste that morning on the bus. I persisted in this ventriloquist/dummy relationship with myself for several years. I was extremely self-conscious.

Together, Frankie and I formed a conspiratorial brotherhood to torture Father Lynch in retribution for his meanness of spirit, for his affected lisp and pomposity during our formative years, and in reprisal for our own imperfections and weaknesses which we were compelled to confess to him.

It was Colucci's thinking to put a mixture of hashish and crack cocaine in Father Lynch's censer, a brass vessel used for burning incense during Mass.

Getting it in there for Lynch to smoke up the church was the work of a friend's altar boy brother. He was an impish prankster but still expected to be paid. Raising the money for a couple of high school kids was the primary problem, as was arranging for the purchase, through layers of underground intermediaries, which tripled the price.

Lynch did his best to parade up the center aisle of St. Patrick's, swinging the little brass bucket on its three-pronged chain. He flicked and retrieved it smoldering through the air back into his brain with the ignited, finely ground dope to illuminate himself, the altar boys, and whomsoever of the parishioners got a significant enough whiff.

Lynch got as far as the tenth row before he buckled into the granite aisle to examine, in hyper-empirical detail, the potassium and feldspar, quartz, and other elements of the polished stone beneath him. He was taken as suddenly to experience, in stunning technicolor, the Brutal and Glorious Second Coming of Jesus Christ, Lamb of God, roaring down the aisle toward him with bared teeth, accompanied by horses, lions, and locusts with men's faces in sparkling Green Rainbows, Crystal Rivers, and the Red, Red Blood of Babylon.

The altar boys pranced in the new free-flowing smoke, pointing and laughing at the ladies in their newly fashionable pillbox hats.

For months we were forced underground while police and diocesan investigators were determined to find and prosecute the perpetrators of the now famous St. Patrick's Censer Doping. One of our friends whittled information from his cop-father at the 69th Precinct about how things were going, which was intense.

Frankie and I fashioned ourselves heroic brigands exploring existential freedom in a senseless universe we molded to our solipsistic desires. But we needed more money for future operations. Mostly, we needed psychological support.

Eddie Costa was easy to recruit into our ring. He didn't have any money, but he had audacity, and his knowledge of the early existential works of Dostoyevsky and Kierkegaard were invaluable for reassurance.

And Sartre! "Existence precedes essence." We interpreted this to mean, "We could because we did" or "We did because we could," although it surely meant something else.

We were arbiters of our actions, determiners of what would accrue from this idiotic trick versus that childish stunt. As Simone de Beauvoir approached her fifty-second birthday, we plotted our next caper—the release of pigeons at the Offertory from behind the altar stone. No problem for us.

Visions sparked in our heads of Lynch cowering inside his vestments as birds flew Kyrie Eleison, Christe Eleison in coils around the high ceiling of the church, where they would roost and coo and drop pigeon-guano onto the pews, parishioners, and blessed statues of the saints, angelics, and godheads below.

But The Rising of the Pigeons ran into cash and logistical

problems that caused us to pull out at the last moment. What we actually did over the next months was plan. That was it.

Plan or dream of future operations, both efficient and untraceable, until cash magically arrived. For example, the holographic projection of Our Lady of the Narrows over Father Lynch's head at High Mass; the tape player attached to Saint Patrick's statue exclaiming in exaggerated Stage Irish the saint's dreadful need for "a pint of the dark and a piss" after his years affixed to the spot near the side wall; and the introduction of helium into Lynch's lungs prior to his Sunday homily.

Despite our tireless planning, scheme after scheme failed to materialize due to unforeseen circumstances until we conceded we were scared shitless to do anything and came to acknowledge—we were existentialists of the armchair variety.

After conferring for several months what to do next, we decided to attack the enemy by taking a more passive-aggressive approach. We would take the struggle to Father Lynch at his weakest point—confession.

Confession provided certain First Amendment and ecclesiastical protections and anonymity from prosecution, while fulfilling our internal, existential being and will to power. What we did was offer Lynch ridiculous sins of medieval sensibility after scanning Pope Gregory's finely defined cardinal sins. We made a list.

We were guilty of avariciousness and cupidity. We were vainglorious and slothful. We confessed to being bored or desultory or disinclined to act.

We suffered from despair and ennui.

"Father, I moped around the house last Friday."

We kept idols and were prideful: "Father, I replaced St. Joseph's statue on my bed stand with my baseball trophy."

We were lascivious: "I got impure thoughts sticking my tongue in a donut hole, Father."

We coveted creatures of the field, air, and sea: "Father, I desired to drop goldfish into my underpants."

Maybe Lynch was on to us. We were ridiculous enough, yet he seemed sufficiently engaged.

It was clear he loved confession Saturdays, loved the aesthetics of the great hall of the church and the powerful things that happened when he uttered the words.

What we said hardly mattered. When he spoke, he flared at us like a rat testing the wind despite his possibly good intentions.

My thinking was, he got caught between what he was saying and what he was hearing himself say, causing feedback loops and distortions inside his head. The slightest lisp would set him off like a whistling tea pot. Nevertheless, we knew the power and the glory were his because the miracle only cracked when he snapped the whip. Deinde, ego te absolvo a peccatis tuis—Therefore, I absolve you from your sins—in nomine Patris, et Filii, et Spiritus Sancti. Amen. And it was done both here on earth and there in heaven, because he said so.

Frankie and Eddie were content to play along with Lynch on the ecclesiastical merry-go-round. Unfortunately, I was not.

When I was sixteen, I left the silly games to them. I went to confession to Lynch every Saturday. I marched into his confessional, often jumping in front of old ladies and children with easier souls.

"Bless me Father, for I have sinned."

Then I'd say something absurd or depraved. What Lynch was thinking behind the screen looking into the wall meant nothing to me.

"I cursed at my mother," I told him.

Then I told him the function and the purpose of each phrase and word, the mechanical and the intentional cause of each look, each feeling in chilling detail as if I knew, which of course I did, even if it wasn't true. Also, her reaction and mine to her.

What was truth but the friction between perception and memory? My mother died when I was five.

I confessed: "I touched myself, Father, while a pretty girl petted a cat on a stoop and pretended it was my... you know. It made me so sick I swore to never again. I did this sixteen times a week since my last confession. For these and all my sins, I am truly sorry."

I tried him every Saturday, week after week, with my most pathetic impulses. He would comment. Or his mouth parted as if to speak, staring into the wall.

I told him I lied in my previous confession. "It was about something I didn't do, that I said I did. I know it's a sin. I don't know what to call it." I asked if I could borrow against future sins, since "I already confessed ones I didn't do. You know, establish a Lynch escrow account."

"Father, I had intercourse with my sofa last week between the cushions but couldn't ejaculate. I pretended it was Mitzi Gaynor. I kissed the pillow of her face until I did."

I kept at him every Saturday. He kept sitting with his face to the wall.

A month into my new campaign, on a day howling clouds of brown and gray turned the holy statues pale, I walked into Lynch's confessional in front of a seven-year-old girl in the pew with her legs wrapped around herself in examination of conscience.

This time the confessional screen was already open. My little act was over. I was unavailable to give a shit. He looked at me directly through the partition for the first time. He got tipped by somebody from the parish. Or he figured it out. Perhaps he always knew.

I smiled a "take your best shot" Brooklyn smile, indicative of both disdain and amusement.

Our family's situation was well known. "Michael Lafferty," he said. I talked to him off the record, now that the pipeline to heaven was severed, of my inversions, of my searching, and the snakes which continued to writhe in my dreams. How they surrounded my bed, hissed and rattled if I tried to escape, how sometimes they let me walk over them, like the Virgin stepping on the Serpent. How I made fun of him and his lisp. Of my counter and my counter-counter-selves.

How my mother committed suicide. He said "Yes" to each revelation because he was Father Lynch. And because he already knew what happened to my family.

"Of course, my son," he said.

I said how we were raised by our sarcastic, wonderful father after our mother's death when we were five, three, and one.

How the family were traveling in the black Plymouth to Coney Island, kids squeezed in the back seat for a day at the beach and the rides, hot dogs and sky—me, the oldest, in the middle. Perhaps it was undiagnosed postpartum complications or bipolar discord little known to the medical profession at the time of her passing out the car door. Perhaps she was so sad she couldn't stay.

How my mother opened the passenger door and stepped onto the Belt Parkway at fifty-five miles per hour.

"Goodbye," she said. The coffin was closed.

"Yes, of course. I know, my son. I know of your family's

great loss. God's forgiveness reaches to all of His children," Father Lynch said.

"I'm not your son."

I left it at that and was down the side aisle heading to the front of the church before I looked back.

He was out of his box, watching me pass the marble reliefs of the Stations of the Cross descending from the Fifth Station of Veronica Wiping Jesus's Face to Number One where Jesus Stood Condemned by Pontius Pilate for our sins.

It was the first time I felt bad about something I said or did in a long time.

When I got to Our Lady's candles near the altar, I used a wick to borrow a flame from a candle lit to implore another heart's petition—to light a candle for my mother.

The snake was, as always, under her foot—and the apple was, as always, in its mouth since the statue was cast. Since her Son died on the Cross for our crimes. Since the original sin in the Garden.

I knelt under Mary's statue so we could see each other better. I told her about the snakes around my bed. How they were now in my head more than her Son was.

"Step back, Mother, please, just an inch," I said, loud enough for Lynch to hear if he was there, loud enough to reach wherever Mary was, although I knew she was stuck in time and plaster by the same people who put her and the snake there to begin with.

"Let the poor thing be. Let it slither where nobody can see its suffering as much as everybody else is."

A small group of parishioners had gathered around me looking up at her and the snake, as if I was speaking for them, which I was unaware—or they perhaps expected her to speak to me like I was Saint Bernadette at Lourdes or something.

I suddenly had enough and headed for the front doors past

Fathers Lynch and Smith, who were both standing in the aisle outside their confessionals.

I ran to the park to have a talk with my dad, who I hoped was there, to be among God's pigeons. Either way, I had a confession to make.

Blood Lovers

"We can't give you love
and rhetoric without the blood.
Blood is compulsory."

—Tom Stoppard

Ninety-Second Street
Bay Ridge, Brooklyn, NY
[1964 — 1976]

At the haggard edges of New York City, the Fourth Avenue Local of the RR Line started or ended, depending upon your intentions, at Ninety-Fifth Street on the far ass-end of Brooklyn, where the city skyline was but an aspiration. You could barely see the Statue of Liberty if you were on a rooftop and knew where to look.

Rosemarie Zuccarelli and I wedged against the front window in the first car to watch the rails expand in parallel fury into our rattling images reflected in the glass, at the horizon of something without explanation at infinite speed. You could forget where you were going, forget your name, forget what you meant.

On Wednesday of Easter Week in 1964, eight of us from the neighborhood took the subway into Manhattan to catch a matinee the girls really, really wanted to see—a semi-religious movie about early Christians.

Previews featured Saint Peter nailed and crucified upside down, played by a melancholic, terraced-faced actor looking up through a pasted-on white beard defying gravity. Weeping supporters craned to capture the drift of his remarks. It was a corny, Academy Award moment with comic appeal, so we headed for the city.

After too long at the window, we staggered to the nearest

pole to let a bunch of little kids press their fates into the magic mirror. I came out of my reflections to find Rosie's hair wrapped around the pole and her cheek. Her shoulders rose as I freewheeled a one-handed hold that swung me over and into her at rolling intervals. Something what I guessed a long-term relationship was like.

When space opened near our friends, we floundered over and flopped ourselves down on extruded green plastic seats that ran up both sides of the train. In our parents' more intimate day, people sat on wicker seats facing each other, often knee to knee, a few feet away. Not us.

Always adjacent to the direction we were going, we were incidental to the movement; a package to be transported sideways like a carton of eggs. Optimal sitters and standers. Optimal eyes deferring not to stare into the eyes of strangers along the other side. Bulkheads, reflections of track fires, red lights and green lights, and local stations flickered across the opposite windows.

Sometimes a train full of passengers would roll by from an adjacent world in the opposite direction, at double each other's relative speed. I caught sight of two people I imagined were us, oscillating in black and white on the other train before it sped away. I grabbed Rosie's hand to keep her in my peripheral view. A Miss Subway poster and a transit system map caught our interest a moment before a sleepy unconsciousness came, leaving our eyes open but turned off on our prefab benches. The heads on our shoulders bobbled like being rocked to sleep in the dancing bounce of our mothers' arms.

Time was on a free pass when we were stunned by sunlight, flying out of the tunnel into the mile-high sky on the Manhattan Bridge over the East River. Our every sense was electrocuted by splintered strobes cast by daylight through bridge cables and stanchions, rattling at forty-eight m.p.h. into

Broadway Station, New York, New York. The guys jerked around all afternoon. The movie stunk, even when Peter was crucified on his head in 3D to symphony music.

"Did you like the movie, Mickey?" Rosie asked on her toes.

She spent a lot of time up on her toes. She, of course, loved it, even if it stunk—because it was her and her girlfriends' idea. It made them holy. I avoided the browns of her eyes. I hoped to preserve her goodwill with an upfront, amiable lie. It wouldn't be the last.

"Sure," I said.

There was enormous purity between us, but the world of desire was magnified by possibility. Rosie and I were truly nice to each other, unlike typical teenage boys always after something, or girls that wound up hurt no matter what boys did or didn't do. Ever since we were ten, we deferred to each other, yearned behind Venetian blinds, and shared soda bottles like proxy kisses.

We were the best distance runners on the block, great for street games. Better for when the whine of a police car responding to a burning stack of Christmas trees would set the local kids and teenage toughs scattering through the streets. Rosie and I, captured by the crackling flames like early hominids amid popping sap and flying sparks, would bolt, weaving around each other like foals.

Our hearts strained out of the neighborhood to walk lazily home, comfortable enough to not always talk. I kicked cans and stones along the sidewalks and our hands perhaps touched, fingers hooked—our secret—one shared by the dogs in the street and every kid and parent on the block.

Through the winter months, sewer gas rose from each intersection, dusk to dawn—four furnaces of steaming fumes, not quite sulfurous, but opaque, drawn pale-white from the depths into the darkening air by the physics of hot sewer and cold air.

It gave the neighborhood a miasmic quality, as though out of the pages of Dickens' London.

Sometimes I'd disappear into the sweep of a sewer cloud, trusting blind intuition to jump onto the curb or forget myself in the rush of the rising steam to linger, as if I belonged, to be assailed by imaginary beasts and whirlwinds I overcame with wit and wizardry. When I emerged, she would be halfway up the block, and I had to catch up with an excuse or another, like, "I dropped my change" or "I got talking to the Devil and got dizzy."

It was a weakness I needed to work on.

We went to different schools. September through June our relationship depended upon meetings to and from stores or the launderette or mindless street games, like I Declare War, that we lived for. I never declared war on Italy; she never opened hostilities with Ireland. Sometimes we would skate-surf holding onto back fenders of trucks waiting at the stop sign on Battery Avenue. Rosie was the only girl who would do it. Her girl-friends skated with iron rods up their butts on the grindy side-walks from side to side, flailing their arms for a stability they found impossible to achieve.

If Rosie and I were clever or lied, we went to Mass without our families. Once, we sat together, breathed the cloistered air with each other's breath in it. In the middle of Mass, Father Lynch mumbled his way in Latin up the center aisle in unyield-ing, brightly colored vestments like a fourteenth-century Arthurian green knight. With sandals hidden, he floated as if a galleon with unfurled green sails accompanied by a pair of altar boy sloops.

Swinging a brass censer from a chain, he thickened the air with burning incense. Too heavy to easily dissipate, it spread in viscous apparitions through the church. The smell stayed in a person's olfactory soul until death and possibly beyond.

Once, as we knelt together in our pew, her hair touched my shoulder and sparkled down my arm like a living thing in the stained-glass light, the heavy musk of censer smoke, the secretive Latin, and the promise of life everlasting. I winced with joy. I wanted to live inside her. I wanted to be reflected in her eyes, bury my face in the unwinding curls and starling tints of black and copper that were Rosie's hair.

The good thing about being in love at thirteen was, not much was expected. This had to do with Brooklyn, the times, and my particular family. But authentic "birds and bees" talks in the average mid-twentieth-century American home was a rarity.

That year my stepmother Margaret got her hands on a book from the parish, Listen, Son, by some priest about sex and adolescence, and handed it over. I was desperate for a crust of insight or any sliver of anything to do with carnal desire. I read it in a day, parsed each euphemism, sifted each Latinate term and ecclesiastical evasion for clues. Nothing doing.

My first hope for clarity came when Vinnie Di Paolo got "the talk" from his father. Italians were more advanced in these matters. He planned to tell the guys all about it as a civic and humanitarian duty. Movies and TV stuffed teenage boys' dreams with adorable Haleys and Annettes, but we would be clueless what to do if we caught one.

Early Friday. Schools were off for Flag Day, although there were no flags we could see. Kevin Dolan, Eddie Costa, and I, and three or four others sprouted around Vinnie to receive physical love's secrets in a remote corner of the broken-glass-and-weed-pervaded lot behind the candy store.

We sat on rusted wheelbarrows and paint pails. Slender paths, grooved hard by bicycle wheels and the feet of dogs and running kids, cut a minute off the walk around the block. I dreaded what Vinnie might say.

I saw a photo in a book where sperms swarmed like tadpoles around a large orb; another showed a wing-shaped, headless harpy holding an egg in each outstretched hand rising from the well of a woman's stomach. What these objects had to do with each other or me was a grave concern.

Rain from a recent downpour dripped from the milkweeds and thistles in the undergrowth and trash. Low thunder growled in the east over Canarsie through the Rockaways as Vinnie spoke. He spoke well, using his hands and sneakers to emphasize key points. The idea that came across was that the penis and the vagina were both involved, but the actual topography and instructions were as murky as ever. He said there were passageways and folds inside a girl's vagina that could be negotiated by a penis if there was a hard-on.

"Next, you'll have a wet dream," he said, "even though you weren't asleep."

We looked at each other. There were no questions. I was a confident kid, but to slip through the drawn curtain of the vagina seemed unlikely.

After Vinnie's speech, Eddie, Billy Olsen, Kevin, and I hung around a remote part of the lot under a dead elm tree. Our mood was solemn. I had a penknife. We did not discuss what Vinnie said. We took turns bouncing the knife off the tree. Twice, Eddie got it to stick. He had cerebral palsy, which gave him the requisite randomness of athleticism.

Then we became blood brothers. We saw it in a movie. Although the implications were vague, we knew it called for a ceremonial mingling of blood. We knew it was secretive and an unbreakable bond—Brothers Forever.

No one remembered the blood brother words, nor whether there were words, but our belief was that the event was sufficient to enact the bond. A dry run proved index fingers optimal for interpenetration of blood for four. Poking, not slicing. Kevin stabbed the point into his finger without expectations and fell thrashing on his back into the dirt. Twice I tried to push the tip in. I held my finger sideways, closed my eyes, and jammed the knife home into my fingernail.

"Mother of Christ!"

Hot darts of pain shot up my arm. Rather than sacrificial, brotherly blood—a red-black hematoma radiated under my nail from the cuticle like a sore, bleak sunrise. I sank next to Kevin in the grass.

I passed the thing to Billy Olsen. He knew there was no way, so he made the quick decision—he told me years later—to shield the operation in the crook of his midsection turned to the elm tree. Even Olsen knew he was a pussy. Screaming, he stuck the knife into his belt buckle.

The three of us were now whining like dogs on our knees. We knew immediately. We should have made Eddie go first. Even at thirteen, Eddie Costa was fearless. Except when it came to himself. He could kick you into the harbor off a pier, stick a rat down your pants, or goose your sister, but his mother had to sedate him to give him a bath.

Eddie started whimpering with the knife in his hand. There was no discussion whether the ritual had to be voluntarily entered —like marriage or suicide—so I wrung loose the knife. He was about to have one of his seizures, so Billy Olsen knelt on his arm while I cut his fingertip with a twisting stab. We pulled him up, and with blood pouring out of at least two of us, intertwined our fingers to spread the gore. It was meant for life. There was enough blood for a dozen blood brothers. Erections were unavoidable.

We evaded going home for lunch and headed to a park where we climbed a tall tree and straddled branches like imagined horses, did nothing, and thought about things we didn't share. Eddie sat on the ground against the tree trunk, sobbing about something. Kevin pulled off a leafy branch and dropped it on Eddie's head.

"Hey Eddie. How ya doin' down there?"

Noon Angelus bells sounded faintly from the surrounding churches, not so much to call the faithful to prayer, as to spread the afternoon's growing drowsiness.

Word spread through the neighborhood what we had done. Mrs. Costa was furious. My dad adjudicated harsh punishment to keep him on the good side of my stepmother, who was hearing it from the neighbors about "the poor spastic boy." No dessert for a week, extra duties, and cancelled privileges. We negotiated terms sitting on my bed. I got the impression I was to put on the dog-face around the family, take out the garbage for a week, and dry the dishes. No shooting hockey pucks at the Johnny-pump after dark.

I sat solemnly at the table looking at four translucent bricks of green gelatin, the most unlikely of human foods, while everyone but me ate. My father and I exchanged meaningful glances. My sister Maureen lifted a surgical spoon tipped with Reddi-Wip toward her lips. She said, "Yummy," which sent the Jell-O quivering. I was occupied by Vinnie's talk most of that year.

A few weeks later after dinner, while I decided what homework I could put off until morning, my dad in unaccustomed nonchalance hung around the table fussing his hand through his hair.

"Mickey. Ah. How's the book we got you coming? Wanna talk about it?" I knew very well my father had nothing to do with the book. "Nah, I read it. I'm good."

"Any, ah, you know…"

"Questions? Nah. I'm good."

Together, we watched my stepmother's abandoned

cigarette by the sink circulate smoke spirals in dissolving, helical patterns.

A forensically perfect band of red lipstick on the filter left imprinted the cliffs and crevices of her lips.

My father, still fretting with his head, was the first to summon himself. He was disturbed I swallowed the book in one gulp instead of stopping at the early-teen section, a workup to the "self-abuse" masturbation section, then on to the late-teen chapters on dating and marriage, concluding with a glossed-over, secret reproductive act referred to as an "embrace," and a never-ending march of infants into the octopus-arms of the Church.

"I'm still a little concerned," he said. I was concerned about everything—the book's lack of factual "how-to" detail and its disregard of the humiliating questions left unanswered.

A year previously, I awoke one night to hear my stepmother and dad coming out of the bathroom trying not to make noise, laughing, saying things I didn't understand. I thought now was the time to push him.

"Dad?... Never mind."

Why bother. We both knew my stepmother was hovering within earshot. Everywhere in our apartment was in earshot, and we perceived the smoldering cigarette to be my stepmother Margaret herself.

We sat grievously at the table. She sat a few yards away out of sight in another room on a second-hand, champagne-colored sofa. We knew her disposition. Her shoes would be off, stockings draped over them like snake castings.

An empty wooden dish for "dainties," she called them, was on the coffee table with her feet. She lit a Kent and used the dish for an ashtray. She had a lump in her throat that wasn't necessarily there. My real mother died when I was seven. My siblings and I were a little hard on my stepmother sometimes.

She was alright, I guess. Everything in the room, including her, tilted toward us in the kitchen in the waning light, slanting from the ocean through the front window.

"I'm good," I repeated and shut up, but I had a question—the only question, really: Hey Dad, if I wanted to do it, you know, with Rosie—like you and her in there—how would I go about it? I may have been ignorant, but I wasn't stupid and was beginning to understand the answers to life's essential questions were not to be found at home. A look came over my father, like he knew something was wrong between us.

"What's troubling ya, son?"

I was about to cry, I think—although I would never.

"Oh, that," he said like he should have known.

He took me by the shoulders over to the stove. He did not play it up. "If it happens so in life, just present yourself. She will understand because it is her body after all. She'll put you inside her and there you'll be happy as a clam. Tight and safe and out of your mind in paradise. The female is the greatest creature created by God."

We hugged a little and moved back to the table.

"Wanna egg cream?" he asked. That night, I smiled myself to sleep—dreaming about Rosie putting me inside her.

It was summer again and everything changed. Rosie walks became routine.

The days and nights were long, and the young owned the streets—from toddlers toddling along sidewalks to full-blown teenagers kissing, smoking, and God knows what else, singing in acoustical doorways.

I remember when the turning came for Rosie and me. It was late August after two hot, blazing months in the streets. The poor squirrels were stuck half-lifeless to the telephone wires, their little chirpy mouths silent for the first time in their lives with their tails hanging limp. The gang sat on a stoop sniffing around for a shred of sophistication and we'd get trapped in an endless loop you'd need a German dictionary to have a sufficient word for. A squirrel came crashing dead in the stifling heat onto the street and that was all anyone could stand.

Vinnie suggested ring-a-levio to break the cycling boredom of Brooklyn and the butt-dragging, hazy afternoon. And that called for girls.

It was not clear why ring-a-levio called for girls, but girls kept the two teams' "jails" filled, and their screams carried subconscious sexual tensions we were only vaguely aware of. It was a game you were compelled to play well through puberty. More fulfilling than the more democratic spin-the-bottle, it was a run-and-tag game so simple, with defense flowing back and forth with captures and releases, and the only time constraint was dinner. Two front stoops served as jails where the captured were held unless freed.

Rosie and I were always on the same side and when she was captured—Ring-a-levio One, Two, Three—I would lead coordinated attacks on the enemy jail or lone suicide missions to free her. Despite her whippet speed, sometimes she got caught on purpose.

On that day in boiling August, during a brave game of ring-a-levio, I threw myself rolling under a black Chevy Bel Air near the enemy jail, which was Junior's stoop.

I smacked my head laughing on the asphalt street, pulled myself face-sideways through stones and grease, and waited on my cheekbone for the jail to be loosely guarded. There was a lot to be learned about life from ring-a-levio. Patience. Loyalty. The feint and the false stride. Self-sacrifice. Love.

I crabbed behind the car to run around token interference, stomped on the stoop's steps and grabbed Rosie's arm, Hump

Free-All! The magic words to set us away together down Battery Avenue where we might linger until dusk.

She said nothing, grabbed my arm, and slapped me in one burning motion across my face. She may have punched me. Just as determined, she jumped, kissed me on the lips or thereabouts, and ran crying up the block into the vestibule of a building she did not live in.

I imagined her pressed, clouded in uncertainty against the hallway wall where a tin-silver panel of mail slots with small, irregular nameplates and buzzer buttons gave what solace they could as she wept. She may have been laughing her head off for all I knew.

I sat on a step on Junior's stoop-jail, intent upon the cliffs of the three-story house across the street where Rosie lived with her parents, aunts, uncles, and half of a small Italian town. Pigeons lived as high up as possible, wanting nothing to do with us unless we had something to eat.

They shuttled by each other in the late afternoon sun, pausing to allow their bodies, which they left behind at each step, catch up to their heads. Several males cock-danced, spinning fandango like Spanish gentlemen with puffed breasts and fanned tails, to burrrrrr encoded messages to indifferent females.

Hens busied themselves with trifles along the ledges or gathered in small meditative groups. One pair, with pigeon desire, was about to do it near a sandstone gargoyle of a winged angel. The cock had problems, faltering several times on the hen's back. He tried naïve, sliding thrusts across her tail before strutting off in face-saving bobs and twirls.

All along the ledges, young males danced, and females napped or fiddled with straw. It was as close to a formal birds-and-bees lesson as I would ever get from a fellow creature. I remained long after mothers called out their windows Raa-alph and Bruu-uce to dinner. A freshening breeze from the surrounding sea ruffled the feathers of birds facing east, and blew maple seeds in green gyres over Ninety-Second Street. Sitting there, the seat of cognition shifted to my thorax, where it remained on and off for my teenage years.

I waited until my father searched out a parking spot down the block before I crossed the street to join him in climbing the stairs. I never told him. I never told anyone. I never touched my face.

Over the next week, intelligence came in gossipy guarantees that there was trouble in the Zuccarelli household between Tony and his wife Angelina that had festered many months. Squabbles and arguments were heard in Italian. She couldn't take the way he looked at her, the way the neighbors looked at her. She was persecuted. There would be a face in the Zuccarellis' third-floor window. Something like a face. Something there and not there.

I would be walking up the block or loafing, looking at birds heading for trees before dark, and there would be a woman with long, darkening hair singing into the pane. I could not hear her song, but it was unbearably sad—I could tell by the way her neck trebled and held the notes, how she peeled back her head to the gray sky. Over time, I gleaned from neighbors she was "not well" and perhaps drank too much vino "more than occasionally."

When Tony got home from work, he took care of everything: Angelina, the money, the house, and Rosie. I spent afternoons on Junior's stoop where Rosie could see me from her window dark and still behind the blinds. The neighbors treated me like a wounded animal.

The afternoon before Rosie Zuccarelli left Brooklyn with her mother to live with her maternal relations somewhere in the Midwest, she joined me on the stoop. She asked me to take her to the elm tree. She held out her thumb and said, "Please."

Her thumb was pinkie-small. I ran my penknife across my finger. I could not cut her. She could. We kissed whatever brand of kiss we had and pressed our thumbs together to form a strange bird that fluttered in pain before us.

In the morning, she was gone. We were thirteen. Then we weren't.

Rosemarie metastasized into likenesses and lies, was diluted by adaptations and revisions I fabricated to fill forward the missing frames.

In the years after, I did what teenaged boys did.

I played sports, pushed my luck with unassailable girls, snuck beers, and cheated on tests. I wrote poems. Spare poems I did not share, poems touching upon alienation and nothing-ness, the depths of the surrounding black and unyielding ocean, and the silence of God in the world.

It was my habit to stop by Zuccarelli's Market after school or if a date didn't go so great to see Tony, who always had some-thing to arrange at the market. He would shrug or grumble in Italian if I asked about Rosie. As far back as elementary school, I would see Tony in the neighborhood or at his market.

We would talk about practical matters like the weather, locations to display fruit angled in boxes, or how girls were. He'd give me a pickle for the walk home and unpronounceable vegetables to bring to my family: zucca, radicchio, and cavolo nero. My stepmother wouldn't touch them. I had to wash them and peel them. And if anyone was going to eat them, it was going to be me.

"I seen those Guinea women pulling the filthy weeds out of the dirt in the lots," she would say.

Meanwhile, she served up cans of waterlogged, grayish waxed or string beans and peas with more water in the vegetables than vegetables in the water. My father said Tony and I had a mixed-up rapport—him absorbed by the workings of the world versus me daydreaming about the causes and effects of mysterious things I knew very little, if anything, about.

Since his family left, Tony took book on the side to keep life moving in front of him. He was not happy alone. Cars pulled up at all hours. Add foot traffic and kids on bikes doing the "bookie run" for the old man, and the market hopped.

He was not alone even when he was alone. Birds followed. When he couldn't see them, he could hear them squawking and fluttering. Blackbirds of all types: starlings, grackles, and crows —but sparrows and wrens went along too if caught in the flow. Birds would follow us tree to tree if we walked home together. He said it had to do with a family curse.

"I have nothing to do with them. I don't like birds I can't eat," he said.

But the birds were entertaining and were, if not happy themselves, hyperbolic, frolicking, and nipping each other through the foliage. He was content, I could tell, to be around them, the way he bent to the racket.

When summer evenings settled in, Tony and I would sit on wooden produce boxes watching mosquitos float like willful dandelion seeds over the discarded vegetable bins—moved by "fermentation currents" according to Tony.

It was then Tony lit the cigar he had slobbered on since noon. Sizzling smoke rose blue-white in the unhurried air to float mournfully through the neighborhood. It was time to discuss matters of critical importance: Animal Magnetism, the Allegory of the Cave, Anti-Matter—deep enigmas he untangled in rhetorical twists and phrasings of his hands, perhaps trying to impress me.

He would lean to squint over his cigar with a half-face like a cubist portrait before his final word on any subject: "How many angels can dance on the head of a pin?" or "Who wins a race between Achilles and the Tortoise? It ain't Achilles! Why's that?"

The focus of his erudition led me to believe he obtained his repertoire of knowledge through Volume I of a supermarket encyclopedia: Aardvark to Axis. I'd get a Coke for the walk home. When I started college, I stopped asking about Rosie. He never said anything anyway.

The day after four Kent State students were shot dead by National Guard soldiers, a woman from the old country came to live with Tony: Teresa Maria. She came with a nervous condition and Coco, a lapdog. The details of the transaction were unclear, but for months, the sun rose and set, cloudless over Tony's Market. His letter "A" speculations were replaced by nuggets he shared from heart-searing romance novels with promises of mortal sin.

Tony introduced marigolds and geraniums to the market in red and green foil-covered pots. He made little effort to sell them. He would say, "Signora Magnani, I put in your bag a little fern for your windowsill or stoop."

Some plants he named. He'd say, "Ciao, Luigi!" to a geranium, or say to a multi-flower arrangement, "Mr. and Mrs. Christoforo, how's the family?" He added tulips for Easter that he spelled "t-w-o-l-i-p-s" and carnations for Mother's Day—red if your mamma was with you on earth. White if not.

He gave the white ones away, if someone tried to buy one. He said flowers had souls we could smell. All summer, fans blew souls of flowers through the market, and we walked home under blackbirds. We had things to discuss—how love was and the circle of life. It didn't last.

Teresa was a lovely woman, but quickly sank into dipsomania. Like Angelina, she neither cooked nor cleaned the house. Tony did everything after work, including pick up the empty wine bottles. He had his fill of her in a few months and spent more time at the market than usual, which was a lot.

Months became years, Teresa dug in, and I graduated college—summa cum mediocre. I had a lot of things on my mind. One afternoon, I stopped by to see how Tony was doing.

"So Tony, what's up?"

"I have something to show you."

It was a boa constrictor in a wooden box in the back room of the market. It was about four feet long and thick as a fire hose with gray and light pink spots and bottomless black pearl eyes. It waved its tongue every few seconds in the succulent market air. It would be considered beautiful if it wasn't Brooklyn and it wasn't a boa constrictor. I could see it through the slats. Tony said it was still a baby.

"You're so smart with your gravity and clock-wises. What do you think?"

"You're going to sell it? You're not going to eat it. I don't know, Tony. Teresa?"

"You're a smart boy. I'm just waiting for the snake-quarium or whatever you call it to come and I'm taking it home to live with Teresa and me forever after. I've arranged for mice for it to murder and eat in the living room."

There were a lot of things Teresa hated: work, sobriety, breathing outside air. But Tony knew his woman when it came to large, killer serpents.

"Tony. You are a genius. What's its name?"

"Don't need one."

"Of course it needs one. Something terrorizing, like Fang. How about Satan 'The Constrictor' Zuccarelli? Give my love to Teresa."

Still, I felt bad for Tony. Why not just tell her to leave?

What could she do? It was like Tony to show his soft side by giving his live-in girlfriend a boa constrictor—a not so gentle nudge nevertheless.

It was ten o'clock Friday night a few weeks later after another not-so-great date. I was on my way to Mulcahy's for a couple with the guys and stopped by the market to see how Mr. Satan was working out.

"Hey, Tony!"

I was going to get into why the sky's blue or how come steel boats float, but I could see Tony didn't look so great.

"Hey, kid. No discussions why dogs don't fly tonight, okay? Remember Satan? It ain't Satan no more. She calls it Dion. She moved it into the bedroom. She likes its slanty, snaky eyes. It slithers up her leg and flicks its forked tongue on her neck. She gets drunk with it and I don't know what else. I sleep on the couch."

We didn't say much. Tony screwed with some dead-looking vegetables. I told him a joke I figured he wouldn't get, and he didn't. At least he didn't laugh.

On my way home from an early evening with another girl who didn't share my concerns over the expanding cosmos, I stopped by to see if Tony was still on the job.

There was a commotion of grinding walkie-talkie static, and lights of police cars along the avenue coming from Zuccarelli's Market. I ran. Cops prevented gawkers from getting front row seats of the dead and dying. I thought I saw Tony half under a canvas bag.

I darted around barriers and cops to find Jimmy the Smirk, a drunk we knew from around, ripped apart by bullets. Flowers in red and green pots were scattered. A cop turned me by my neck into the floor where my top eye caught Tony being wheeled off on a stretcher. He saw me the way a drowning man sees the sun. I was pulled up by a cop who knew me from Little League. "Go home, Mickey," he said, and got me to the street.

I sat on the curb watching corpses removed in body bags and forensic guys collect shell casings and embedded bullets in fruit and vegetable crates into morning. They paid no attention to the marigold and geranium souls with people's names, yellow and brown, nor noticed the "twolips" and red and white carnations honoring mothers littering the floor.

Tony never made it in life to the hospital. NYC papers ran stories, mostly with archival photos of guys coming out of courthouses and clubhouses with faces covered.

The next day when the cops and technicians left, I hung near the market as flowers were taken home by people stepping over yellow crime scene tape—one each, two per family. I spun around to face an unmistakable sound. Cloaked in linden trees across Third Avenue, black crows and iridescent grackles gnawed at their feet.

Tortorello's Funeral Parlor overflowed with Tony's extended family. Market customers and compulsive gamblers came to glom their respects on the deceased. Several overweight pashas in black suits and pinky rings sat in guarded corners, surrounded by semi-wise guys whose necks circled in their collars, waiting to be acknowledged by or inspect this or that person of interest.

Tony was compelled to smile in his coffin with the help of undertaker's sutures and wires. His colorized, matte peach lips reflected favorably in the gloaming of his coffin.

His "beloved Teresa Maria," Father Lynch called her, in his summation of Tony's "Life in Christ," was up front, shit-faced. The family acted as if she wasn't there as they greeted associates and loved ones. After the first night, Tony's brother Angelo shot Coco in the chest and had Teresa sped to the airport with a one-way ticket back to Napoli.

At the Last Viewing, there was stirring at the back. The room hushed when a woman in black, about my age, appeared in the doorway escorted by gentlemen from Tortorello's.

She had a miniature Sophia Loren thing going on with three-inch heels that gave her a jittery equine look before wobbling toward her father's face. Her deep black-brown eyes were highlighted by vibrant shadows of silver and cinnamon-blue under penciled eyebrows. Her lashes were long and waxed to accentuate a crown of high, raven-black hair. Surely Rosemarie, just not necessarily the girl with me under the elm tree at thirteen.

Guided by her elbows to her father's side by a shuffling cordon of cousins and uncles, she collapsed to the floor. After fanning her with a newspaper with a photo of her family's market on the front page, "No Leads in Market Slaughter," she was able to weep in front of the father she hadn't seen in eight years.

I copped a ride with Rosie's cousin Leo to Calvary Cemetery in Queens—the resting place for three million Catholic bodies sans souls, where Tony was mourned in ordered ranks by blood, organizational status, and incidental friendship.

The final processionary, performed by a blackness of elderly women versed in the ancient Italian grieving arts, inched toward Tony with moans and choral sighs to toss or let drop red roses in the vicinity. The women fell onto the grass where they remained until removed. I melted in with the family on the way out of the cemetery to walk near Rosie. I wasn't sure she would recognize me, so I introduced myself just in case.

"Hi, Rosemarie, I'm Mickey Lafferty. I'm sorry about your father."

"I know. Thank you," she said. Her hand glanced off my forearm.

I wanted to ask if I could see her later, but the timing was so wrong, and I was unusually nervous. However, the Zuccarellis knew how Tony and I were and how I was about Rosemarie, so Angelo said, "We're going out to eat in the neighborhood. Come with us." I squeezed into a limo next to a weeping woman who did not stop.

We went to Maniago's, a family-run ristorante with great food and poorly painted murals of villages under steep cliffs on the lapping Mediterranean. I rehearsed what to say to Rosie while making small talk with the family.

Dinner took forever. We exaggerated Tony stories. He shot a man dead in Sicily. He jilted a countess and worked on location moving sets for Fellini. I told them about his blackbirds, which did not make much of an impression. Rosie was contemplative.

The funeral party, if that can be said, was making way for early dinner customers, when I got a few minutes alone with Rosemarie. She looked like a small movie star. Perhaps my right eyelid spasmed. "So, how have things been going for you and your mom?" I asked.

"I'm working at an upscale clothing store in St. Louis, after some wasted years after high school. Just bad choices. Mom passed a few years ago."

My social intelligence was having difficulty inside my mind with inputs and outputs I luckily didn't articulate, when out of somewhere, I said, "I missed you." I waited for her to speak. When she didn't, I made it worse. "I said I missed you."

"I heard you the first time. What am I supposed to say?"

"I don't know, I'm not you. I looked for you on buses, in

parks, among people crossing streets. I'd turn on a whim and you wouldn't be there. In church, I felt you next to me, but you weren't. My dates weren't you."

"That was my fault? I'm sorry. We were kids. I stopped being a kid a long time ago, Mickey. I tried not to think about Brooklyn. And I didn't. There wasn't much to remember."

"I remember."

She took the long view of me through her high, right eyelid.

"I'm sorry. You must be tired and in shock and here I am, pestering you. Look, let's sit in the back. Catch up. I'll walk you home."

We weaved around tables to a spot under another bad mural of an idyllic Italian village with women hanging wash from terrace windows.

Mr. Maniago, sorry for her loss, bought us complimentary shots of anisette. We fell into the warmth of the liqueur, but the blandness of cliché and stranger-speak was still with us. Windows cracked open in my head with little Me's sticking their heads out to apprehend what I was going to say or had said, or what she might say or had said already.

I had no clue who said what, so I told her how Tony spelled "twolips" and how he thought flowers had souls people could smell. I detected slight gaps in her battlements, so I added how her father and I would hang out to discuss matters of mock-philosophic importance, like why clock hands go clockwise, but if they went the other way—would that be clockwise? Her sketched eyeline pushed into her forehead. Up close, I could see her black beehive hairdo, as I hoped, was not of human origin.

She said something too softly to hear, with perhaps a smile

too tiny to notice. I pressed her hand to the tabletop. She thought I was angry.

"Stay in Brooklyn where people love you," I said, "where you have family. You could be yourself here, where you come from. Please."

"I already am myself."

She looked at the mural to cast a cold shoulder. I had to admit, her dispositions and comebacks were deadly and she knew it, so I resorted to bullshit.

"Something happens when you're thoughtful. Like a direct link opens to you inside. Your body gets still—but you would be thinking with your eyes. They'd move ever slightly. Just your eyes. I know things about you. About us."

"What? What are you saying?" She adjusted her bra strap through her blouse.

I measured my odds being close to nil, so I said, "Your eyes. They're adorable." I said this as sincerely as possible.

I didn't think her eyes in contemplation were that adorable. They gave her a medicated, injected look. There were lots of things that were adorable, just not necessarily that. Her stifled yawn with the squinty cheeks and chickpea nose were adorable. Her As If stare was not. But that's what she did, so that's what I said.

Surprisingly, she turned to send a perfectly performed, double-eyed twinkle through her flicked false lashes straight into me that made my heart stop—like the snap shut of a penknife.

It was 6 p.m. She had an early plane to catch. We walked down a steep hill from Fourth Avenue to her uncle's house, next to where she used to live with Tony and her mother. I grabbed some of her fingers to fiddle with. She had a child's hand. Her high heels brought her face just above my shoulders, not counting her hair. But she was not a child. She was Rosemarie Zuccarelli, born on the 30th of May 1971, a woman complete, walking down Ninety-Second Street toward Gatling Place with Mickey Lafferty.

The Verrazano Bridge was built after she left Brooklyn. Its red warning lights blinked in the sea fog, leading cars and trucks over the black waters of the Narrows out of the city into America and vice versa. Air conditioners strained and cycled above empty stoops, which used to be filled with neighbors and used as backstops for stoopball games.

Sometimes it was weeks before you would see a neighbor. Not a dog was on the streets nor a cat under the sky. Neither were children's Skelzy courses cut into the macadam, nor chalked Potsy boxes on the sidewalks. The Brooklyn Dodgers abandoned us for L.A., Yogi retired, and the Sixty-Ninth Street Ferry was shut down.

At the side door of her uncle's combo garage/basement, we kissed like the thirteen-year-olds we used to be. No probing tongues. No grinding into each other. I pulled away to see her face. Rosemarie looked up, surprised to find me looking down at her. I closed my eyes to kiss her again, but she grabbed my tie, which hung dissolute from my collar like a donkey's tail.

"Come. Tell me another lie," she whispered and pulled me into an interior scene from an Antonioni film with dark intertwining rooms behind doors and walls on the garage level that smelled of sausage and gasoline. Her wig was off. Her hair was unruly, which I liked very much, and her feet were bare. I took a blind step.

I held what I could hold—a thigh, a hook of elbow, a clutch of hair. She grabbed my hand. We sensed our way into the darkness where we fell over padded seats and settees, up and down stairways to nowhere. No retreats. No lies. She was not a woman you could prepare for. She was holding me when a thing came over us with deranged speed with no word for. She kept me tight to her through graveyards, mountaintops, and fields of stars until we broke through whatever barriers there could possibly be between two people.

Two hours later, I was again outside her door. Changed, yes—utterly. But also bound, tethered by rudimentary laws I did not understand which now applied to me.

Instead of the safe course home only a few doors down, I walked up the hill and turned left at the market still wrapped in yellow crime-scene tape to find a corner at the bar in Mulcahy's.

On my way, "A Dream Fulfilled Is a Dream Lost" was what I came up with. It sounded profound, which was a bad sign. I allowed for its deconstruction as I pulled a beer across the bar. The exchange of coin for beer was highly recommended by urban philosophers and barkeepers for psychological and meta-physical repair.

The shrink got fifty dollars for fifty minutes. Father Lynch got us to lie for nothing. Mr. Mulcahy got twenty-five cents. My dream-fulfilled aphorism boiled down to: the fulfillment of sexual love was a dream destroyed by the weight of its own success, which was an overly wonked way of saying: I had been a virgin all these years in self-defense against the tumult of sex with one of the local girls—which would have rained down such guilt, such marriage, such low-backed white wedding dresses with hovering bridesmaids and the Hokey Pokey—it would have been insufferable.

But Rosie was no ordinary girl, and the dream hypothesis boiled down to: Why was I so terrified by the woman of my dreams, and what was I doing in Mulcahy's?

None of my buddies were there, just old fellas bent over in layers below the smoke line. They nodded serially and I nodded back in a rolling "nice to see you." Mr. Mulcahy wanted to know how today went. I shrugged. "Remember Tony's daughter Rosie from the neighborhood?"

"Can't say I do." So, I gave him the Dream Fulfilled essentials.

He leaned over for a closer pass, "Mick, take some time off. Nothing rash. Whatever yer thinkin', you'll think different in the morning." He could fold a customer into a safe nook for the night and tie a bow around it. It was his business. The mornings after were ours.

After another couple of beers, I was half out the door when he said, "Listen, Mucker. I wouldn't wring myself too tight over dreams."

He meant it, or he wouldn't have said it. The landlord's dog I played with as a kid stopped barking when I came home, acculturated to the rhythms of my routines; maybe he couldn't hear. I felt his eyes waiting in the dark of the basement.

I made "Hey, Rex" under my breath and walked up the stairs. My stepmother was smoking in the kitchen, humming nonsense melodies over a crossword. I never knew what to call her, so I called her nothing. She was a good woman. My dad would be home from the pool room any minute. It was his night.

"Everything went well. We had dinner. I had a few with the guys," I told her.

Some beers were in the fridge. I grabbed one, helped her with her puzzle, and touched her hand before going to bed. My brother Brian was in our room snoring off his Friday night in the park. I slipped next to him on top of the covers with my clothes on. I vowed to take Mr. Mulcahy's advice. Maybe take Rexy, king of the cellar, along for his first and final road trip. I would be drafted in six months if I didn't land a teaching job, which was unlikely.

Late the next morning, I headed up the block to see if

Vinnie was up to lending me his car, when I was struck by someone looking moony at me, with a little brazen puss, high up on the steps of Junior's stoop.

Rosie missed her flight. She decided to live with her uncle's family, next to the house she grew up—where people loved her, where she could be herself even though she already was. We sat with the electrified eyes of birds thinking of what to say. We hadn't a chance in a million.

"Wanna go for a ride?" I asked.

We addressed our travels to nowhere in particular. For four weeks, we searched America without expectations through zones we marked off inside us.

The first week we made love and thought of little else. I would wake to find my face in her hair, or we would be tangled up in each other in some other way before heading off to find where the next miracle would occur.

We made love in cutoffs adjacent to minor roads in the grass, in open air and multi-leveled parking lots, underwater in public pools and beaches, across the passenger's seat and from behind the driver's, over the speed limit.

Twice, we made love at outdoor concerts on the tips of my toes as Rosie slid down the hood like a fluttering angel. If the Love Zone was all sex, the next internal frontier had us visiting local monuments and museums: the Museum of the Tractor, the Pez Museum, the Museum of Barbed Wire, the Museum of the Museum.

We took in battlefields along Highways of History where deeds were recalled on metal plaques, toured the humble homes of dead billionaires, hypocritical churchmen, and politicians. The Sightseeing Zone was not a welcomed addition, even with residual lovemaking, but nothing like what was to follow when it merged into the Zone of Everyday Life. We brought it on ourselves. Or it naturally happened.

The grind of the road. The meal on the fly. And particularly, the questions I would ask. I asked her about one her father and I tangled with to pass an afternoon while I was in high school.

"Why don't we fall off the earth when we're on the bottom?"

"What are you saying?"

"I'm saying why's that so? It's a kind of gag, like why's the sky blue or why does God let unborn babies die? What do you think?"

Later, we were driving on another tedious highway of history when I asked, "How come iron boats float, you think?"

"What do you care? Ever been on the Staten Island Ferry? Well, I got news. It floats."

"Yeah, but why?" And more. She was a woman without irony. I was a metaphysical man in a physical world. After almost a month, we were back on Ninety-Second Street exempt of heart, head, and cash.

While we were away, Rex died alone in the dark and was put out with the garbage. If I were home, I would have buried him in a lot somewhere with a little cross: Rex, King of the Cellar.

I lived for a while in the room I shared with my brother while I looked for work until drafted, which would be soon. Rosie lived in her uncle's basement, three doors down.

We would almost cross paths, or I would slink up the block, lost behind a false smile. It wasn't that I didn't want to talk to her. I just didn't know what to say. And what I might have, I knew wouldn't be enough. Most nights I watched the bar towel rub across the counter's grain at closing.

Mr. Mulcahy was a man of precise, effective flourishes and

unusual knowledge. He supplied psycho-social sessions late evenings, if the trade was thin. He summed it up, "You think too much." As summer slumped into the somber blandness of autumn, I snuck beers into our room for my brother and me each night I could.

One night we sat at the foot of our bed looking out the window at the figure of a man we didn't recognize in an apartment across the street illuminated by television light. His face flickered as scenes changed on The Tonight Show. Brian said, "Plato's Allegory of the Cave."

I looked at him. We always knew what the other meant, even if we didn't say. There was no way I could sleep with shadows of sense impressions bouncing off some loser's brain across the street, with Rosemarie three doors away. But I did.

In the morning, I looked out our window to find her arranged in the high shadows of Junior's stoop across the street. I walked over with my hands in my pockets. I knew I would have to say something. I didn't know if I liked this woman, but I knew I desperately loved her.

Rosemarie was pregnant.

"Zia Annette thinks… knows," she said.

She missed her period was the obvious thing, but Aunt Annette brought Byzantine skills into play that were extant among Neapolitan women. Magical, errorless senses of smell and taste—the bounteous signs in the urine and follicles of hair.

Rosie did not like being pregnant. It made her "clogged." She was "bloated and swoony" before throwing up in the morning. I wished she would let me rub her back or kiss her, but she didn't like being touched. But please would I hold her, she'd ask, "Just for a while?"

I knew as soon as I did, I'd never let go.

I learned the rabbit dies whether the girl is pregnant or not. For our part, we followed the rules we knew. I thought first about what I was going to tell my father. He had a story for everything. Maybe he'd make one up. Instead, he told me to take a walk up the block to see Uncle Angelo at the market for a one-on-one.

"Don't think he didn't know everything before you did," he told me. "It's not like it's gonna be a surprise. That you're still alive is probably a good sign."

The next day, I walked alone up the street to the market. Since the Verrazano Bridge was built in 1965 and the houses and lot across the street were built up, the neighborhood was in the process of being re-zoned, torn down, built up, condemned, sided, repaved, or slowly transitioned to slick highway entrances and industrial-chic, high-rise apartment buildings with elevators on the avenues. I wished it was Tony and not Angelo.

I would have bought the best Italian cigar I could. We would have talked old times and made fantastic plans for Rosie and me. Perhaps discuss the nature of "Hinduism" from Volume IV of the encyclopedia he'd be reading. And proper names for babies: Anthony or Annette. Angelo explained the rules. There were rules.

I wasn't listening, but Rosemarie would explain later. The meeting went okay. Later, I visited an army recruitment office downtown to see about getting deferred because of the child. No chance unless we had twins.

I reported back to Rosie. She said, "We'll be okay when you're away. I can stay with my uncle's family. It used to be my house. Our house."

We put our best faces to it.

I walked to Mulcahy's to tell him what he already knew. Everybody everywhere knew. My money was no good.

"I take it you enjoyed your trip with Tony's daughter. Congratulations," Mr. Mulcahy said.

"No secrets on this street," I said.

"Between secrets and friends, you're better off with friends," he said. "Listen, Mucker. Unless you're lucky enough to be gay or otherwise queer, or become a teacher tomorrow, or a minister—being a priest ain't gonna work for you—you'd better double up looking for a reserve unit with a short waiting list."

"I tried that. It's Marines or nothing, except they're into killing and dying for their country, which is out of my comfort zone. I better get married first. Angelo says he'll talk to Father Lynch to arrange a 'wartime' quickie."

So began a race between my selective service number which was in the one-hundreds, the Marine Corps Reserves which was a cinch, the birth of Anthony or Annette Zuccarelli-Lafferty, after a ceremony at Saint Pat's—probably not a Mass even though Rosie wasn't showing—and a reception at the Knights of Columbus if the Sons of Italy was booked.

The last night I spent as a single man in my parents' apartment, with vows in the morning and a few days' honeymoon on Coney Island before the bus for Parris Island, Brian and I were having a couple of quarts together in our room.

I spotted a few of my brother's pre-teen Sticker Books piled in the corner: Mammals of the Americas, Migrating Animals of the World, Reptiles! I read in one how many animals, herd mammals, birds, even butterflies, navigated home using an inner compass guided by magnetic fields around the earth.

If I awoke anywhere but in that room, whether I was in

boot camp or stationed somewhere, I would have to wait until the spinning stopped before I could figure who and where I was, like I was some migrating class of caribou.

A few days later, on my last morning in Brooklyn for a very long time, I awoke with my feet intertwined with Rosemarie's aimed west toward America at the mouth of New York Harbor. We opened the garage door to her uncle's house to find the sun had drawn shadows of the rooftops onto Ninety-Second Street.

Vinnie soon came to drive me to the induction center somewhere in Jersey, where I began several years of being someone else.

It would have been nice to have had a Sticker Book of Rosemarie to take with me. A page of her dressed for church in her shiny black pumps showing the décolletage of her toes bunched on top. Maybe a sticker of us running down Battery Avenue far enough to be alone, one of us in her uncle's garage the first time, and a last one of Rosemarie on her toes looking up at me, our thumbs together under the elm tree.

Life apparently provides stickers for fools to paste onto their lives.

Heaven's Door

"If you gain, you gain all; if you lose, you lose nothing. Wager, then, without hesitation, that He exists."

—Pascal's Wager, 1658 A.D.

I didn't know him that well. I shouldn't have even written this. Brother Kyron was our Bible studies teacher. I was our nosey-ass ace reporter on the high school newspaper, The Clipper. My specialties: basketball, track, and indiscernible religious anomalies. What backstory I needed to research I mostly got from the Akron Beacon Journal. My two buddies, Eddie Costa and Vinnie Di Paolo, and I were there when most of what happened, happened. I was there at the end.

Our Lady of the Narrows High School
Shore Road, Brooklyn, NY
[March 8, 1965]

2:00 p.m.

Brother Kyron sat under three rows of fluorescent lights, a breaker to a tide of boys rushing into Room 215 to our assigned seats.

He was forty-five years old, was overweight, and had grown unattractive in black. As a young man, he had spun the metaphoric wheel of fortune, with his life on the line, over the existence of God. It was the only question worth asking. Either He is or He isn't.

Kyron's ante? His vocation to the Teaching Brothers of the Holy Cross in the service of the one, holy, Catholic, and apostolic Church. And if God turned out to be a howling gargoyle or nothing at all, or a Presbyterian, well, Brother Kyron would be dead either way. This much I got from loosely interpreting an interview I did with his parents a few weeks after the incident. Young Bruce, our Brother Kyron, was nothing if not cautious, especially with his spiritual life, or soul, on the line.

Brother Kyron's junior year religion class, The Mystery and Meaning of the Holy Bible, was his latest dodge in the God-game—an odyssey through time, through chaos and order, from Genesis to Revelation to the dismissal bell. But Brother Kyron was no fool. He knew "his boys" had no skin in the game and his class didn't give a shit about his behind-the-scenes motives. He also knew his outlook and teaching style was plodding and dreary, too calculated to appeal to energetic teenage boys after being caged most of the day.

As for Kyron, he beckoned the hours until the day he would learn the outcome of his speculations—one man's life against eternity. He understood he had to be more student-centered, more sensitive to their interests and capacities, even if he faked it. Faith, hope, and charity needed to be performed, not necessarily believed. So, as a practical matter, he waited for the last period on Wednesday to try a more teen-friendly, inter-active approach.

After attendance, Brother Kyron announced the formation of a Bible Studies Club he would advise. It was part of his plan.

"Indeed, the Club will have, as it were, an open agenda based upon student input." But stuffy clichés out of habit attached themselves to his remarks—seminary talk. No one admitted interest in the Holy Bible Studies Club, perhaps they would think about it. (As it were).

2:15 p.m.

"Genesis reveals the very process of God in an emerging universe," he said to start the day's lesson.

What did that mean to a sixteen-year-old? To anybody? He knew no one would show up for his Bible Studies Club. He tried to do better. I looked for things to occupy myself to pass the time. I had the morning paper with the lines for that night's N.Y. Ranger game under my religion book, ready for a peek.

"Let us explore the Story of Creation in Genesis," Kyron said. (Let us stuff ourselves). Kyron stood taller. His head rotated to spray us with preprepared words.

"It takes us step by step over the six days, like a movie short of the creation of the light, the world, animals, and man. Did you guys see Disney's The Living Desert?" He smiled a smile he froze on his face a few moments too long. We either hadn't or didn't see the point in saying we had.

"The time-lapse work? How they sped the seasons into a minute? If we close our eyes"—he closed his eyes—"we can almost picture The Beginning, building day to day until it's a living Universe. Complete. And it's done in a few concise pages. Look."

He flipped the pages of Genesis as if summoning reluctant kittens. He looked around. We looked at our texts. What was the question?

Some boys responded to something by the windows, perhaps a comment behind a cupped hand? Was that a blowjob sign performed by a thumb and a mouth near the door? A sound surely came from the back.

Kyron stopped.

Deep silence. No one dared bring attention to himself. Some snuck back to math or history homework under their religion books—others stifled laughter, or telepathed jokes. I fiddled with offensive and defensive lines for the game that night and passed it on to a kid a few desks up.

The class communicated like prisoners in penitentiary cells through mimed transmissions and pencil-hockeyed notes along the aisles.

A macrocosmic view of the class would reveal Brother

Kyron looking encouragingly at twenty sixteen-year-old boys thinking of what to say if called upon. But a curtain drawn back to reveal the microworld of Room 215—like a placid-seeming drop of lake water studied under a lens—would unveil unimaginable creatures twisting and pulling through the viscous medium of the inner classroom, the merest of treading oscillations reverberating in all directions in stunning purposelessness.

2:30 p.m.

Bro. Kyron picked up the pace.

"Did reading Genesis inspire you in any way?"

We sat, knowing that saying nothing was the shortest course to the end of the period.

"Primitive, pagan creation myths have stories of fighting gods and enormous turtles. Steve Reeves! Anyone see The Clash of the Titans?"

I bet he hadn't.

"'Let there be light and there was light.' That's it! Why just a sentence? Someone?" The kaw-kaw of mid-afternoon seagulls followed a mooring ferry churning into the pier along the black waters of the Narrows across the street. I wondered who they were squawking at and what the point was.

Brother Kyron said, "Whom was God talking to, anyway, when He said, 'Let there be light?' There was just Him." (Whom, indeed).

This question, I assumed, was not in his plan. Perhaps it was a question to hold for his Bible Club or judgement day. Kyron seized upon a random boy.

"Mr. Johnson. What do you think?"

"I'm sorry. What do I think about what, Brother?"

Kyron's eyes ebbed. No one liked Johnson, who was too stupid to fake an answer.

"About anything, Johnson. Genesis, for example. What you had for lunch. Or who God was talking to when he said, 'Let there be light.'"

"That's a good question, Brother. Himself?"

In the back of the room, someone blew an unintended lip-trumpet. I stuck my Ranger doodles into my text and closed it, sensing trouble. Edward Costa, a wise-ass kid who suffered from cerebral palsy, spasmed in a corner seat. His right arm, which was virtually useless except as a kind of air rudder when he walked, began to bend. His IQ was 135, but that was just a base estimate. Edward's state of mind was undeterminable. Whatever it was, it wasn't good.

But Eddie was popular, due as much to his contempt of authority as for the sad circumstances of his condition, which could be comical if accompanied by a sputtered wise crack or obscene gesture. Eddie was one-of-the-gang in our neighborhood, kept us laughing for a decade as kids from the curbside while we played stickball or ring-a-levio in the streets. He unzipped the back of Marianne Ahern's dress in the sixth grade and did MAD Magazine faces outside Sister Teresa's classroom window.

He was attention dependent. All eyes were on Kyron, who chose to ignore Eddie. He jeered down at Johnson. Certainly, learning and teaching were unconnected disciplines.

"But what about the days, Johnson? Do you think it took God six days and He had to rest, exhausted, on the seventh? Like He needed a break? Maybe pull up a lawn chair?"

"That's what it says, Brother, so, yeah."

"That's what it says. How long is a God-day anyway?"

Kyron didn't wait for Johnson to begin his next dumb evasion. He looked around the room, but we had transformed to avoid identification with mental life—a subtle loosening to indicate deficiency-of-being around the mouth—an unbalanced cant of the shoulder or over-glaze to the eye was enough to take us to the other side of sanity. Kyron selected his next boy from this lineup of empty eggs.

2:40 p.m.

"Mr. Di Paolo."

Vinnie was bright sometimes. Kyron took a moment to decide what path to lead Di Paolo down, while he gathered himself to the sound of his name. Kyron picked up the pace.

"Mr. Di Paolo, why does the Bible say it took Almighty God six days to create this world?"

"Because it took that long, Brother?"

Kyron's fist clenched in his cassock.

"Mr. Di Paolo, did you read the Creation section in our text? About the notion of time in the ancient world and in the minds of the inspired writers of the Bible?"

"It said time was different then, didn't it, Brother?"

"You didn't read it, did you, Di Paolo?"

"I did. About ancient times. The sun was kind of faster, I think, back then, Brother."

Eddie Costa entertained a band of boys along the side row, casting an imaginary penis through his fly toward Kyron, reeling it out like a lure on a fishing line with his feeble right hand, while his left angled the pole at Kyron's mouth anticipating a strike.

Several boys near the windows followed a small flock of pigeons on the apartments across the street. All along its ledges, cocks cooed, spun, and danced before hens falling in and out of pigeon-sleep.

"You didn't read it, did you, Mr. Di Paolo?"

"No, Brother. I was sick."

"You were sick."

"My mother wouldn't let me."

"Your mother wouldn't let you."

"Yes."

Brother Kyron invited Vinnie to join him in the hall to discuss the situation. This would not be a slow, drawn-out sadistic affair which would continue minute after minute—the cunning smile, the musk odor of the man over the boy, his volume, his breath, the blackness of him, the cruelty of his eyes.

This was going to be quick but brutal. Vinnie was going to take one, as much for us as for himself. Brother Kyron's doubts, questions, and resentments, along with the accumulated sins and fantasies of all the Catholic boys and all the Catholic teachers in all the Catholic classrooms of the world, were carried by Vinnie Di Paolo and Brother Kyron into the hall. The door shut.

2:45 p.m.

Primarily, Kyron understood the primacy of sound. He would have attacked Vinnie in front of the class if he wanted to create fear or clarity. Instead, smashing Vinnie's head unseen into the wall in the hall would provoke creativity—like the tread at night of a chipmunk across a forest floor became a bear in imagination.

The sounds in the hall of shuffling feet, the rising syllables of unintelligible rhetorical questions and attempts to respond would become amplified in our minds. Kyron knew it would be best if the class heard sobs. He lifted Vinnie onto the wall by his hair and spat rebukes into his face. The stubble of Kyron's beard rubbed against Vinnie's cheek. He did not sob.

The assault would last less than ten minutes. At best, it would lead to a week of superficial Biblical studies and rote memorization. Kyron's hopes of journeying with us through Genesis would sink again into the seething drop—dreams of mortal sins, tits, and cartoonish vagina drawings. I continued plotting line pairings for the Ranger game. Welcome to adolescence.

Eddie never gave it a thought once he spotted it. He rose into his knees-joined, splayed shuffle on the insides of his shoes across the floor, swaying to make progress like a hurrying merman. When he got to the front desk, he held it above his head, then brought it to him like a child to his breast—Brother Kyron's Holy Bible.

"I have Gah's wh-word," he said with articulation difficulties thought to sound.

His voice took time to warm into fluency. He used his diaphragm and lungs to bellow air through his larynx, like a bagpiper with melody and drone pipes pushing and sucking. When the queued-up words began to arrive out into the world, they lagged internally but soon settled into a vibrating rhythm at Eddie-speed through the fine reeds, muscles, and the sounding pipes of his neck.

He opened the Book.

"It says here. At the end of days, when the Seven Seals bark in the seas, the Big Lamb will shout, 'Eat this, Ky-Ron!'"

He grabbed his crotch, shot a lizard eye at the door and then back, then forth at the class.

The intertwining of these events made it uncomfortably

funny and perilous. The absurdity of what was happening, with the full effect of Eddie's disabilities, gave it a Jerry Lewis-like mock-mad quality. Combined with the sporadic thump of Vinnie's head and Kyron's derisive demands half-heard in the hall, it was an irresistible call for rollicking anarchy.

Laughing at the handicapped freed the reptilian brain. Particularly when a mob was involved which included the disabled person. At such moments, citizens stormed soccer pitches and burned orphanages in limbic hilarity. Sober men danced to executioners' songs.

He scanned the Book's early pages, and made contemplative sounds sitting on Kyron's desktop. "Get bent!" he said. He looked up to share insights with the intimates at his feet. "Here's Adam and Eve. How cool is this? Adam's what? A couple of days old? Eve's an ex-bone. Don't eat from this apple tree, God says. There's a snake in it!"

This was what Eddie lived for. Every eye was on him.

"It says here, the tree is the Tree of the Knowledge of what's Good and what's Bad. What does God expect? Adam doesn't know Good from Bad because he hasn't eaten the apple yet. Here's this douche walking around Eden with his girlfriend, dum-de-dum, and doesn't know the difference between right from wrong, so naturally he takes a bite. He has to take a bite in order to know what's right and when he does, he finds it's wrong. He can't win."

The class began to hear more clearly the sounds from the hall, and wander back to daydreams, or hurry to finish homework. Eddie's Adam and Eve riff bored them as much as Kyron. His deal was Jerry Lewis, not Lenny Bruce—so that's what he gave them. He started again. He opened Brother Kyron's Bible to where it was ribboned. Some pages may have bent. I winced, but there was no way Eddie would stop.

"When Moses moveth through the Land of Sand, they

went without food," he said. "God dropped by smoking a joint, 'Hey man. What's up, Moe? Be-eth thou hungry?' Then God declared, 'Let them eat pussy.' And so there was pussy and it rained spaghetti from the sky!"

With that the Bible flew from his hand, splayed face-down, putting indentations in Psalms 75 through 122. Some pages may have ripped. We could see it on the floor. Eddie turned to locate the book as a sound came from the hall. The knob turned. Kyron pushed Vinnie in first, his forehead splotched with red, face snotty, his hair knotted by fist holds. Shocked to see who was on the front desk, he hurried to his seat.

2:55 p.m.

A calmness settled over Eddie, who breathed in and breathed out. When Vinnie saw Brother Kyron's Bible on the floor, he buried his head into his arms.

Kyron paused at the door to orchestrate his entrance, swirling a black cassock around his waist several times in closing the door behind him. He swished forward to face his boys. Instead of twenty reflective souls, he saw Eddie blinking at him on the front desk. His desk. Then, he saw what he saw on the floor.

He moved incrementally in slow motion frames. It was unimaginable. Inside its cover was the inscription: "To our son, Bruce, Brother Kyron, who was chosen by the Lord to help young men find their way in the community of Christ – Mom and Dad."

Kyron bent to retrieve his Bible and petted straight the pages of Psalms. He moved towards Eddie until their noses touched. Ahab eyes searched deep into the unreadable Eddie, who looked back. Perhaps Kyron would tell him to leave, or perhaps Kyron would leave, or find something in Eddie's eyes to indicate purpose or mitigating intent and he would say, "I forgive you as Jesus would."

Kyron straightened Eddie's head with a blow across his face with the front of his Holy Bible, then plugged him across the ear with the book's spine, spinning him off the desk. Kyron's mouth lathered as he hatcheted Eddie's neck which he tried to shield with his withered arm. Leaves of Scripture began to fly into the air from their bindings upon Eddie, Kyron, and the students in the front rows. Chronicles, Zechariah, Luke and Matthew, Acts, Timothy 1 & 2, and most of Romans drifted down. Kyron continued to hack away at Eddie through the flurry of Bible pages.

Eddie was now protected only by his clog shoes raised to deflect the Bible blows, sending more pages into the air, intensifying the co-joining of the Old Testament with the New.

Kyron ripped the book to shreds against Eddie's legs, then pitched what was left at his head like an emptied revolver. Nothing but the initial Creation pages of Genesis and John's Revelation from the Sixth Seal clung to its covers.

I could have been hallucinating as reproductive duplicates of Eddie and Kyron appeared to dance in holographic flourishes in shimmering rage and theatrical immensity in front of the room. But no! Eddie remained fixed on the floor, now totally under the desk at the epicenter of the attack, as Kyron bent over, Bible spent, to sight a knockout uppercut to jaw or chest.

Static clicks came from high on the wall. *Freshmen track practice is cancelled today but will resume Thursday. The Chemistry Club will meet this afternoon for boys still working on their projects.* Hearts stopped. All turned in horror to the gray box.

The Sodality of the Blessed Sacrament will *meet this Thursday after class to plan next month's field trip to St. Patrick's Cathedral.*

Kyron struggled to comprehend, excommunicated from his senses.

All was still in Room 215 where Eddie lay inert, curled on the floor—a broken spider.

Junior Varsity Basketball consent forms are due at the end of the week. I came from the back to gather Eddie but couldn't pull the proper strings to make him rise. He reposed in my arms like a giant puppet, his head lifeless like Jesus in Mother Mary's embrace or General Wolfe on the Plains of Abraham.

3:15 p.m.

The dismissal bell trumpeted the clang of time, and the class rushed for departing buses to rip off jackets and ties, freed like adolescent wolves into the surrounding neighborhoods. I let Eddie roll to the floor. I had to go.

Vinnie Di Paolo, several boys, and I with after-school detention lingered by the door to see Eddie untangle limb by limb, to edge across the floor on two knees and one hand to what was left of Kyron's Bible. He snatched it with his bad hand and continued crawling until he stood looking again into Kyron's eyes, dialed wide. He opened the Book where a few rumpled pages clung and read: "And God said, 'Let there be light, and there was light. God saw that the light was good, and he separated the light from the darkness.'"

He might have kissed Kyron's mangled Bible, but all the boys at the door agreed: like Saint Thomas's hand in Jesus's wounds, Kyron's fingertips probed Eddie Costa's uncomprehending face.

"It doesn't say who He was talking to," Eddie said.

5:00 p.m.

Two hours later, Di Paolo and I returned to our spot by the door. On the desk were Bible pages parsed into books and chapters, New versus Old. Brother Kyron and Eddie Costa sat on the floor holding themselves up with their hands around their knees.

Vinnie was standing in front of Kyron before I noticed him missing. "I want to join your club. The Bible Club," he said.

"That was a bad idea, the club."

"Maybe. I want to join."

Vinnie sat with them on the floor and asked a question that had been on his mind. "Brother, how do you know it happened like Genesis says?"

"The authors were inspired by God."

"What were their names?"

"We don't know."

"Why so many authors when nobody knows their names?" Vinnie pressed. "Why not God tell us Himself how He made the world? Why are things so a mystery, told by guys who weren't there? So filtered sideways? Why's there so many people like you?"

"I don't know."

"Maybe Creation was a mistake. Look at Eddie here. No offense."

"Fuck you, Vinnie. My mother made me read the whole Bible, then made me read it again, while you played stickball in the street. It took a year the first time, two the second. I read a lot'a things. God made Adam and Eve and a Garden and, in a few days, just for being themselves, He kicked them out. Everything is fucked up, not just me."

Vinnie sat next to Kyron, then leaned back on the floor looking into the fluorescent lights with his hands under his head.

"You got some anger shit to root out, you know that?" he said.

"Yes," Kyron said.

Eddie bowed his back to relieve a cramp.

Vinnie summarized his thinking from the floor: "So, we trust guys nobody knows their names with the Story of Creation."

"Yes."

"We have a lot of work to do."

"Yes."

"Tell me," Eddie asked Kyron. "Who was God talking to in the beginning when he said let there be light?"

"I don't know. Maybe He just thought about it."

"No offense, but, how do you know what any of this stuff means? As if you were there."

"I studied. We studied."

"That's what faith is?"

"Yes."

"So, you choose to pick God, God don't pick you. Like choosing up sides for a ballgame."

He shrugged.

5:30 p.m.

The pigeons across the street huddled against the loss of light spreading from the east to the west across the apartment houses and trees. I was about to leave my post by the door to join them on the floor when I heard Brother Claude, the school's disciplinarian, and the principal, Brother Fabian, rattling up the stairs heading for Room 215, their rosaries around their waists rubbing stride for stride up and down their thighs. I ran down the hall to wait for Vinnie and Eddie outside.

There never was a Bible Studies Club. Eddie Costa and Vinnie Di Paolo were expelled the next day. Brother Kyron was told to wait for Brother Fabian and pray for heavenly guidance in the school's chapel. Instead, he went out the front door where he passed our school's patron, a glowering statue of Our Lady of the Narrows balancing a model clipper ship in her right hand. She had the look of a teenage girl turned to stone in mid-breath. Our guiding light.

He walked across Shore Road in the rush-hour traffic heading for the Staten Island Ferry Pier, two blocks away on Sixty-Ninth Street. The ping of the flagpole's grommets in the wind rose metal on metal over the noise of the cars and the ferry horn, providing tympani to the commotion. I followed at a distance like the sixteen-year-old snoop I was.

I was in stealth mode as Kyron moved toward the ferry. The ferry slip was designed as a battering ram for ferryboats to smash into while being thrown into reverse, bouncing side to side by momentum and the tide against the pier's pilings—a giant wooden catcher's mitt, not a dock.

Children on the boat ran to all sides to watch whirlpools spinning around them as the ferry churned to a stop while seagulls cried like flying pigs in hopes of murdered fish and discarded snacks in the tide. I stepped aside for a crowd heading from the ferry dock. When I tried to pick up Kyron's tracks again, he was gone.

Maybe he got on the boat without me seeing him. What would he do in Staten Island without a car? I leaned against the railing to wait for the boat to depart, when I spotted him under the surface of the water. His eyes were opened in death, staring through a curtain of bubbles. His black cassock lifted his arms above his head, giving him the appearance of a man posing himself a question he had forgotten the point of.

In a few minutes, a crowd gathered as ferry personnel retrieved Brother Kyron's body. I walked back to tell Brother Fabian what happened. How Brother Kyron probably tripped on the pier's flooring into the water and hit his head on a pylon.

Some of the brothers were already on their way.

"It looked like he was taking a ferry trip to think about something and must have fell in."

"You think?" Brother Fabian said.

"Yes."

"Sure?"

I nodded.

Being Billy Olsen

"One's real life is often the life
that one does not lead."

—Oscar Wilde

Bay Ridge, Brooklyn, NY
The Jersey Shore

Billy Olsen didn't remember the moment he started to grow into the image everyone had of him. Nor whether other people's "Billy Olsen" was anything like the real one, if there was such a thing. Self-awareness was not a strength. My belief was, he didn't want to be the unreliable narrator of his own flat story arc and was better off being out of it altogether. I remembered because he told the gang everything before he forgot or repressed it, and I was a perfect reporter of his story because I didn't care one way or the other.

"Billy Olsen" tripped through elementary, high school, and college with few rewards or sorrows, perfectly just okay. However, in the early fall of 1974, for two consecutive Thursday nights, his specific problem became the focus of the guys' regular session at Mulcahy's Bar & Grill on Ninety-Second Street and Fifth.

His troubles revolved around the conclusion of his virginity. Even that was to be expected. It was happening all around us over the last several years. How the young women dealt with this problem, we had no idea. Just because it took one from each category—one from Column A plus one from Column B— to form a loss-of-virginity, didn't mean they were helpmates or partners in the proceedings. Complicating matters was the likelihood that one's last virginal experience tended to be—one from Column C [Consummated] plus one from Column D

[Virginal]. What gay people did was totally queer and alien to us, but it couldn't have been any easier.

Roughly half of the children of our acquaintance went to various Catholic schools inside a fog of sexual ignorance. Those who received public educations were not that sexually advanced but at least benefited from going to school with the opposite sex, where there was at least a bare minimum of sexual health information. What did "we" do? We humped each other through our clothes; or scored the occasional, unrewarding coitus interruptus; or got some poor, likewise unprepared girl pregnant, whom we immediately married or abandoned; or were tricked by, or became entangled with anyone who would conform to our desires—no matter how infantile—for the price of a wedding ring and two "I do's."

When safely incarcerated in the bonds we took, we thoughtlessly birthed innocent babes into our little apartments and tenement flats until holy menopause or erectile dysfunction overtook our reproductive impulses rather than reason.

No matter the difficulties faced by the neighborhood guys, nothing was ever taken seriously at our weekly drinking sessions. Sometimes this accrued therapeutic rewards—more often, our situations became worse. From 1968 through 1975, we simply lacked the escape velocity to move out of the neighborhood or find better friends.

The story Billy Olsen told us was re-told so many times it became scriptural. It wasn't something he'd lie about, either. That was another thing about being Billy Olsen. He didn't have the good sense to not be honest all the time.

Billy Olsen was almost twenty-two when Alexandra Schuler, whom he hadn't seen since elementary school, made a crucial re-entry.

After graduating from college, Billy Olsen was employed selling televisions, tires, and brake jobs as a full-time summer employee at an automotive store down the Jersey Shore while waiting to be drafted into the losing side in the Vietnam War. To kill and or die for his country were options he was most reluctant to take. They met by chance on the last Thursday night of the summer season at Big Al's in Asbury Park.

By twenty-one, Alexandra's skinny eighth-grade body had accomplished the work it needed to do—enough, at least, for Billy Olsen. She was still a piece of work in a funny, confident way. Wonderful, lyrical, mystical. She was hot shit and she saw him first. Billy Olsen had a squirrely leg, like a lot of guys. Alexandra Schuler caught him—and his bouncy left leg—alone at the bar, alternately looking into his beer and watching the band behind the dance floor from the bar's mirror.

He was trying to understand why everything going into the mirror, from dancing bodies to furniture, to the guy on drums, came back reversed or inverted or turned inside out because... why? It was a known fact. Even Billy Olsen was the inverse of himself in the mirror in front of him. Alexandra Schuler was untroubled by such matters. She was untroubled by leg-twitchy men as well, but was fully wary of the difference between left-leg fidgeters and right-leggers. Left-leg men were right-hemisphere-driven, non-verbal communicating personalities. A category of man she could deal with. And how.

Otherwise, right-leg bouncers tended to be abstract thinkers, talkers, temporal, rational, logical, linear. Some other sister's dream boy—not Ms. Schuler from Dyker Heights. Not that night.

She had a girlfriend in tow. They headed to the bar for unlabeled twenty-five-cent beers where she sidled next to the stool Billy Olsen and his left leg sat bouncing on. She caught a glimpse of the reverse image of Billy Olsen sitting next to her reversed, together in the mirror.

"Don't I know you?" she asked.

"How can I possibly answer that?" Billy Olsen said with an interested half-turn. His leg stopped. His heart did too when he saw her.

"But I hope I know you," he said.

"Brooklyn, no?"

"Brooklyn, yes."

"High school?"

"All boys for me, unfortunately."

"St. Pat's?"

"I know you. Alexandra Schuler. That's it. I'll be Billy Olsen if you want? We sat next to each other in eighth grade. St. Pat's! We never spoke, I don't think."

He noticed he was strangely witty and calm once he shut his leg off. He was normally overly sincere and on the anxious side with girls, or anyone, really. But tonight was different.

"Right! Only they call me Sandy now. Sandy Schuler. Sounds kind of dippy, don't you think?"

"I'm not saying. I'll let you know later, if I think of something good." He had a sidewinder smile that made the line work. She held out her hand. She introduced her girlfriend, So-In-So. He wasn't listening.

He grabbed Sandy Schuler's hand hello. He bought their beers then took the girls to the edge of the dance floor to be in the middle of what action there was, which wasn't much. He would have asked her to dance, except Alexandra—Sandy—was likely an amazing dancer, which would be a deal breaker for his confidence, now on the high road. And what to do with Ms. What's-Her-Name standing there with her head at a girlish tilt? She was doing a tic-toc move to the music with her knees pinched together for a honey-bunny look.

Normally, Billy Olsen's Column B type girl. But not that night. Not with Sandy Schuler in town. Sandy and Billy Olsen ignored the girlfriend to listen to the band, a mid-week Jersey

Shore band of second-rate Jersey City musicians down for a one-nighter with a front guy behind the mic that had guts and no voice.

They commented upon the dancers, noticed how those who could—mostly girls—seemed to have another person inside them who did the artsy, coordinated work, allowing the actual girl to look at her partner, smile, enjoy the dance, even flirt if she was into it.

Everyone else—mostly all the men—danced with earnest faces meant to impress, taking the long view down a leg, stumbling into unplanned steps they tried to make look intended. Mysteriously Hispanic moves were made by un-Hispanic-looking men in solipsistic, over-the-shoulder glances.

He and Sandy worked well together. Witty, with improv hooks and intuitive complications, they braided together quips and wisecracks. About how friends were. And the immediate benefits of having kinesthesia listening to "Stairway to Heaven." Or how stage lights affect sound waves in the air to the mind and the horrible thing that happened to Billy Olsen when he was in the eighth grade, in the second aisle of St. Patrick's Elementary attempting to read from the geography text.

"What!?"

Sandy Schuler thought he knew. For Billy Olsen, there were only misty memories of hippopotami in the Nile and the Mediterranean shores of Africa.

"That woman, Sister Mary, is dead," she said.

"Oh."

Billy Olsen took Sandy Schuler to the bar where they drank a lot of not-cheap crappy beer. Her friend, What's-Her-Face, purred like a meerkat near the dance floor before mysteriously disappearing. Sandy told him about her memories of his attempts to read from the geography book that day. She thought he was hysterically funny. Then, of course, she knew it was not. But that was okay by her. Everyone knew he was out of control.

"No big deal," she said. I remembered it differently. It was nearly dismissal time. Sister Mary Magdalene gave the order to hunt out in our geography books the chapter on Africa. Some of the countries had pre–WWII European names we wouldn't recognize today: Belgian Congo, French Equatorial Africa, Italian East Africa. Sister Mary didn't care what she put into our heads provided it used to be something, even if it wasn't anything anymore.

A few hours earlier, Billy Olsen had a run-in with one of her prized dioramas—a two-dimensional tableau with two-dimensional cutouts of Jesuit missionaries poaching for Jesus Christ the souls of innocent Iroquois. A solid blue paper river flowed through it in case there were going to be baptisms next to the papier-mâché forest.

She described to the class, holding back barren tears, how she worked into the night pasting, scissoring, drawing on cardboard construction paper, and fashioning goop to look like landscape. That was until Billy Olsen came along—tra-la-la—all sweaty from the schoolyard after lunch with his inattentive post-slap ball-playing arms swinging to rip her Iroquois/Jesuit encounter off the wall.

Father Jacques Marquette lay face down along with ripped Indians and a section of a paper river. What could Billy Olsen say or do? The only thing important to Billy Olsen and me was who was sitting across from us in the third row. Rosa was not-so-hot, but basically, really nice. I liked her very much. Smart and friendly.

She was one of the few girls who would say hello to a person, even if you were a boy. She already had maybe eight primed baby-ovums in her, ready to launch for the right guy in about five years. I suspect Billy Olsen liked her, too. Who wouldn't? Sitting in front of her, adjacent to Billy Olsen, was Alexandra Schuler. Not so bright or sweet, and she would never say anything to any of us no matter what, but she had something Rosa didn't. It's hard to explain.

I'll try.

Girls' blouses of the Catholic school uniform buttoned left over right, like most women's blouses. Naturally, there was always enough space between the fold and the buttons, if you were at the right aisle, for... I'll try again.

Alexandra Schuler wasn't a big girl like Rosa. She was thin and brazen. She wasn't yet hot by nature, but she was braless. Who could tell? The boys directly adjacent in the second row could tell. Billy Olsen and I were fully familiar with the parts we could see. A small but perfect breast. A girl's breast and the curve it made like a pinkish handball resting lightly on top of her ribs. Too cute for words. I suspected she knew exactly how cute.

The procession of paragraphs being read in the geography text slotted one by one up the first row, desk one through desk six, across North Africa west to east. Everyone was in top voice, considering Sister Mary's disposition. Catherine, Michael, Susan—with Tim next, chirping in feigned sympathy for Moroccan, Algerian, Tunisian products into Egypt—and down the Nile.

I read along in the text up the first row, checking out Alexandra here and there. Rosa wore an industrial brassiere like her grandmother. It was then I saw him. Billy Olsen was in front of me, his finger moving across a page he had already identified as his paragraph in anticipation of his turn, which was at least ten minutes away. Reading a section over and over out of context could have only made sense to him. Otherwise, he wouldn't be "Billy Olsen."

While he rehearsed his paragraph, I could see he was

getting more worked up with each repetition, the way his finger returned like Sisyphus up and down the page. The reading-baton passed from Eddie to Susan up the first row to the next child to read in turn. Billy Olsen never looked up, not once—not at Rosa, not at Alexandra Schuler, nor did he ever read along with the preceding kids.

Sister Mary Magdalene said, "Thank you, Ralph. William Olsen, please begin." Impossibly, he was caught off guard! After a flutter, he cleared his throat. He got through the first sentences, when an in-breath met an out-breath and he forgot exactly what to do next. Billy Olsen was now at the extremely overly familiar sentence, "The primary exports of Senegal are gold, oil, and frozen fish." He read something like, "Preemery Seygall, gold, oval and froz flish."

He didn't dare read it again. He struggled with similar results, sentence after sentence. Some would be better than others, nearly perfect, followed by incomprehensible gibberish. His mind and eyes were connected to a web of detours and baffles.

Then, the first kid found it funny. It was Alexandra Schuler. Next, Flip Phillips, a champion glue sniffer from Marine Avenue, joined in as if Billy Olsen's performance was the monologue from The Red Skelton Show. Laughter began to roll up and down the aisles. Sister Mary stiffened.

The more Billy tried, the harder it became to breathe; the more he faltered, the more the kids laughed. Except for me. And, of course, Rosa. Alexandra was gagging in delight across from us. My attention was on her, whose antics might provide hybrid eclipses of herself.

Billy looked over his shoulder as if I knew what to do. Here was Billy Olsen, at the pinnacle of God's creation among creatures of the earth, possessed of mental machinery so effective and complex, so acute and perfected as to be at the top limb of the evolutionary tree, yet unable to complete a single sentence that he had practically memorized for the past twenty minutes. When he got to the end of his paragraph, he dropped his head into his arms on his desk, where no sound was heard. I pointed out to Sister Mary the section in the book I was now prepared to read, when she said, "No, Mr. Dunne. William Olsen, the next paragraph, please. Continue."

His head shot up like Pinocchio called to life by Geppetto. It was the cruelest thing I ever witnessed. It was obvious to someone in Billy Olsen's state of mind that "continue" meant nothing. He began somewhere near where the paragraphs submerged, swam through periods and passages, forded columns blurred from right to left behind a persistent fog. At every marker, he made sounds. I don't think he heard anything he said. No one was laughing.

Not Flip. Not Alexandra Schuler. Not even Sister Mary. Five minutes later, Billy Olsen stopped, closed the book, and said something we took to mean—no more.

"I think it's me, Sister," I said and picked up on a paragraph down the page and began, "Sudan is home to more pyramids than Egypt."

I walked Billy Olsen home. When we got to his apartment, I said, "See ya." He said, "Yeah, Jack." We never discussed the matter again, but I never forgot it. He apparently did immediately. Or pretended to.

For some reason, there in the confines of the bar in Big Al's down the Jersey Shore, at twenty-one, Billy Olsen proceeded to change the subject to explain his eighth-grade fascination with Alexandra—Sandy—and why. What he saw, and what he didn't, across the aisle, which was pretty much the same thing. Amazingly, she found it fascinating, in an early adolescent way. She put her hand on his left knee as he spoke. She had the gift of getting inside a boy's boundaries. Her lashes, long and black, became impossible to oppose—her flesh, young and pure, her concupiscent self in front of him on a pillar of desire.

Billy Olsen was not expecting a guest for the night. Sandy Schuler was not expecting what happened to her, or them, either. Both were conjoined, body to body, kiss to kiss, and Billy Olsen's first time happened in a motel room in Belmar, New Jersey. From what he remembered, in the morning, they made love again. This time both from Column C.

He showered for work, drove her to her motel room in a nearby shore town, and they promised less than half-serious promises neither had intentions of keeping. Well, perhaps he did. She had her "night out" down the Shore, and Billy Olsen was inducted to the world of sexual gratification without having to get married. He told the guys at work about his experience the next day—just not the virgin part. He told it matter-of-factly, like it was a slice of Billy Olsen's everyday life, which fooled no one. While he became an instant mock hero, any hero was a hero to Billy Olsen.

"Super White Boy invade Big Al's for the kill!"

"Slays homey-girl for kicks!"

"Billy Olsen, how's it done, man? I got'a get me somethin' somethin' tonight at Biggie's."

And for a few hours he soaked in the glorious abuse. Two days later, he drove up the Garden State Parkway in a flower-draped chariot with the perfect story to tell the guys at Mulcahy's B & G on Ninety-Second.

But for the moment, he was in his room in the Olsen family's apartment, readying himself to look for a year-round job on Monday. His draft number was 120. Not so bad, depending on how the war was going. The U.S. had just invaded Cambodia. It didn't look good.

By Thursday he was more than ready to tell the guys at Mulcahy's his story, as he knew it, with all the Billy Olsen omissions and additions in the paradoxical way he experienced life.

It was through that personal haze we got the details—results without causes, destinations without journeys, throbbing moans without justifications, served up on misty foundations of speculation. We heard the story from so many angles, we could have testified in court about it.

"She said sounds more than words. Which was good because I wouldn't know what to say anyway and kept my mouth busy," he said. "Nobody took nothing off. Her nor me. We were like totally naked from the start. Which couldn't have been, I know."

He tried to buy a pitcher for the table, but the guys wouldn't let him. They went easy on Billy Olsen that night.

"I was an erotic front-line soldier by the time we did it again in the morning. I had no idea what I was doing."

Except three days later he was having trouble urinating. To the point he didn't want to pee ever again. There was burning. There were discharges. He rang my doorbell.

"Jackie. We gotta talk."

We walked to Mulcahy's where he confessed his symptoms to me over beers.

"Olsen, are you a fuckin' idiot! No condom to be had anywhere down 'the Shore' I suppose? Where they're dispensed everywhere in the toilets for half-a-buck."

"I don't remember. I mean, I didn't have one."

"What are you going to tell the guys?"

"I don't know. Nothing. Unless you do."

"And you shouldn't be doin' beer, either."

Naturally, Thursday night he told us everything. It was perhaps the funniest thing we had ever heard, until it stopped being funny anymore, like most things he did. Billy Olsen's course of action was obvious: get to a doctor A.S.A.P.

However, if you were Billy Olsen, nothing obvious was simple.

For one, the source of the infection was clear as there was no doubt of his original virginity. He also had no doubt there were just two of them; therefore, the guilt ratio of Sandy to him was exactly 1 to 0.

"The bitch knew what was up. Get a shot of penicillin and buy a package of freakin' condoms for frig sakes," Vinnie said.

He opened his wallet where an oval mark was etched in relief by an unused condom.

"I'm not proud it's been in its wrapper as long as it's been, but it's there."

I would have told him pretty much the same thing. Move on. Forget about Sandy. Be prepared next time. Congratulations. And that was what Billy Olsen intended to do. End of story.

He received the number from Special Eddie Costa, who was acquainted with every doctor in Brooklyn. Billy Olsen saw the doctor the next day. His diagnosis was immediate. His prescription: do this, don't do that, here's a shot of penicillin, come back in a week. Billy Olsen didn't remember the doctor saying anything about the party-of-the-second-part, Sandy Schuler.

A few days later, Sandy got a phone call.

Billy Olsen tried but found it impossible to believe she would have had sex with him, or anyone, if she knew her situation. Or, alternatively, he was afraid she would call him first for some reason, knowing he was such an asshole. What he did know was, there was some brand of anxiety or embarrassment involved any way he thought about it. So, he did the only "Billy Olsen" thing he could think to do. He searched the Brooklyn phonebook. And according to the version he told me, he got through on the first attempt.

"Sandy? It's Billy Olsen."

"Bil-ly. Ol-sen." She flattened each syllable to impersonalize him, if possible.

Perhaps he would go away.

"How have you been?" he asked.

It was hard for him to speak, but he opened up about the latest kids from their class to be drafted. Perhaps she already knew the truth about herself.

"Did you hear about Ives? Missing in action somewhere? Once the 'gooks' get to know him, they'll send him back."

He wanted to say straight out, "We have gonorrhea." Or say something equally dopey, "You should get a check-up. I'll pay," like it was all his fault. But it didn't matter what he actually said, because he told me he thought he might have said, "I have 'the clap'."

If that's what he said, it was no lie.

Little things from his heart fell out while waiting for her to say something. There was silence on the other end, but not as long as the silence that followed. Sandy Schuler hung up.

Finding her apartment the next day wasn't difficult—ringing the doorbell was. In all his hanging-by-a-thread existence, there was nothing to prepare him for what happened next. When she opened the door, he flew into an immediate outburst of assumptions.

"I'm sure it was me. I must have picked it up without knowing. Let me pay, if...

I have a doctor on Eighty-Sixth Street we can see, if you want, if you haven't already seen someone, that is. I'll drive you or we can walk."

Ms. Sandy Schuler hated him more sincerely than anyone before in her life. It was awful enough to have a venereal disease, which she more than surmised a few days after their encounter. Now Billy Olsen was on her doorstep. She was also low on cash. Everyone was low on cash. She might have to ask her mother. Maybe Sandy could lie. But how do you lie about that? Lie to her father? Lie to the family doctor? Eventually, she knew.

"It was probably me," Billy Olsen repeated with such conviction she knew he had to be either a total idiot, the greatest douche ever, or a really sweet guy willing to pay her doctor bill. She understood her guilt, but it wasn't like he put up a fight. There was a Column C & Column D thing involved, and she couldn't have known.

They walked to her doctor's office on Seventy-Eighth Street the next day, whom she decided she would have to trust.

"It doesn't matter who's to blame," Billy Olsen said on the same topic along Ridge Boulevard. "No one's to blame. I probably should see the guy myself; for a second opinion, would you mind?"

"Do you believe, let me get this straight—do you believe that I'm gonna walk into my family doctor's office with you? Do you really think so?"

"I can wait outside. I already got a shot." When her visit was over, he paid the bill. They walked the long way back to her apartment.

"We'll be out of action for a while, you know?"

"Did you say 'We?' I thought I heard you say 'We?'"

Nevertheless, she let him take her to the Dyker to see The Godfather Part II.

For Sandy, there were worse ways to be "out of action." He was kind of smart-sweet with Billy Olsen hair; and Billy Olsen's take on life had a "you had to be there" quality that was not totally unbearable. Perhaps even kind of adorable, in an unorthodox way.

While they were out of action, he took her for long walks, to the movies, and the Harbor Diner for hamburgers and

Cokes, no beer to keep peeing to a minimum. Sometimes they snuggled over the arm of their theater seats and often she would tease him.

"You ain't supposed to get hard-ons in your condition, you sex fiend. Get over there!" She'd point to his seat. Or she'd poke him in the dick with her finger for laughs. Nothing in his life was ever like being teased by Sandy Schuler.

For his part, Billy Olsen explained aspects of his boring new job and intimate features of his up-in-the-air life to her as if she were actually "with" him and interested, which she wasn't. Or he would write poems he knew not to give her for fear they would surely have opposite the intended effect.

Life with Sandy in it was living on eggshells of inadvertent consequences. Life without her was not life. He would always say too much, always give her the poem with the purply adverbs he promised himself not to, always confessed the secret he meant to keep. She would likely laugh at him as if she was the thirteen-year-old in the third row and he would pretend everything he did was meant in jest.

He felt better "down there" within a few weeks after another shot, but it was another month before she got her medical "all clear." In between, it was Chinatown, The Exorcist, The Towering Inferno, and their absolute fav, Young Frankenstein followed by meatloaf, or bagels with lox and cream cheese, topped off by ice cream sodas at the Bay Ridge Diner with eight-inch slices of cheesecake.

Besides planning things to do with Sandy while "in recovery," Billy Olsen's only hobby was Thursdays with the boys at Mulcahy's. For all the supposed bravado of young men's bullshit and blather sessions, there was almost nothing the guys said to Billy Olsen after "How's you and Sandy doing?" The unstated strategy was to acknowledge Sandy's existence, leaving unexplored the venereal situation and the course of his expected, certainly soon-to-be-achieved heartbreak.

Talk tended to turn immediately toward the upcoming football season and how the military draft was marching through the neighborhood. Timmy Froelich was home from Nam with a metal plate in his head for brains. Vinnie Di Paolo was going for his physical next week. This was his night to be rolled home in a laundry cart in case we never saw him again, which happened to Bobby Hackett.

Meanwhile, Billy Olsen took Sandy wherever she would consent to go: bowling, ballgames, picnics, and to the circus at Madison Square Garden.

One Saturday afternoon, Billy Olsen took Sandy Schuler to the Dyker Theater to see Cabaret, which they liked very much. Afterwards Sandy wasn't feeling so great. Perhaps her spirits were dragging. They decided to take a loop around Shore Road to get the most out of her sadness, which Billy Olsen insisted they experience together.

The co-mingling of river and ocean lapped at mid-tide against the black rocks and bluffs as if to affirm the drowsiness of the day. She was cold. He helped her arrange her jacket around her shoulders and tucked in her hair, which was soft in his hands.

They walked along Fifth Avenue, then paused at the corner of Ninety-Fifth Street and Fourth for Sandy to say something she had to say. He saw the shadow of the town fall away in the late afternoon down the hill through the streets and parked cars, the houses and apartment buildings, past the church and the melancholy façades of the school and the convent. "What? I'm sorry..." Billy Olsen leaned in. Sandy was saying something.

"Cynthia Overmeyer. Her name? Billy? You remember

her. From that night down the Shore? She told me she likes you."

Crickets geared up nearby in their mechanical, autumnal buzz, like ten thousand tiny bells scraping inside brass bowls.

"You'd be good together, Billy. Cynthia Overmeyer?"

The crickets stopped and restarted, as if orchestrated by a maestro behind the garbage cans in the alleyways. Billy Olsen tilted his head, closed his eyes. He felt the underground ripple of the subway beneath his feet and the bored drone of the highway to the west, next to the river.

"Oh Billy. Oh, Billy Olsen."

Special Eddie

"I must confess,
I lead a miserable life."
—Ludwig van Beethoven

Showtime
NYC & Environs
[1972 — 2010]

I'm Jack Dunne, City College School of Journalism, Class of
'71, Ninety-Second Street, Brooklyn. I was a natural-born
newspaperman—self-proclaimed.

I was twenty-two and owned a fedora my father gave me as
a joke. I swore I would wear it if I ever became a reporter on a
real paper. By the time I did, nobody but the old newspaper
lions wore hats, and I didn't want to look like a jerk. I had other
journalistic affectations.

Even before my first college assignments, I hammered
nonstop on a black 1940s Royal typewriter with tap-tap strokes
from the opening line until the end, like I was playing some
species of piano with typebars flying into the paper and flying
back into the well—clack, clack, clack. There would be an unfil-
tered and unlit cigarette under my lip—my mother wouldn't let
us smoke in the apartment.

The rhythm of the beat with the jam of the carriage return
helped the words grow into sentences, sentences into paragraphs, paragraphs into stories. The sound was the message,
and the meaning kept the pace, and so I wrote until it was a
wrap—clack, clack, clack.

Also, I was curious as hell. So, when in the summer of '72 I
was asked by a popular New York City tabloid to cover the

Third International Special Olympics in Los Angeles on a last-minute freelance basis, I jumped at the chance. I received a round-trip ticket, enough for a couple of nights in a cheesy hotel, meal money, and a healthy slab of on-the-job training.

My editor said, "Just give us the gist. What makes these people tick. The retards. The folks in charge. If it ain't enough cash for you, we don't tell you where to sleep or what to eat."

I took the assignment personally. Eddie Costa, a friend almost from birth down the block, had cerebral palsy, so I was naturally interested. I couldn't imagine him running a race or playing basketball. Eddie wouldn't lift a finger for anybody but himself, but we appreciated how he made fun of his friends or anyone else if he felt like it. I also had a cousin with Down syndrome who said she had a boyfriend she loved truly, not that he was aware. She wanted one so badly—she loved him, she said, "with all my heart." She was a sweetheart.

I also had a natural need to know how come a crippled girl dragged herself inch by inch on crutches across a track in the rain to finish last by fifteen minutes in a "special" foot race. Why a kid with muscular dystrophy picked up a discus or a blind kid ran into the darkness. Even if I couldn't figure out what made the spark inside them burn, I could write about what it looked like.

I found a case for my Royal, the paper lent me a camera, and I hopped on the first flight to L.A.

My article didn't win a Pulitzer, but it was enough to earn regular work as a stringer when assignments popped, and they did—a lot:

"Beached Whale Draws Crowds and Flies to Coney Island."

"Human Foot Found on Flatbush Construction Site."

Crime, politics, sex, and disaster stories went to the regulars. I was more than happy to cover the leftovers.

"Endangered Imperial Penguins Hatched at Bronx Zoo." — Jack Dunne.

Still no Pulitzer.

A few months into my new "position," I was in the Komedy Klub on Eighth Street in Manhattan, down the block from the paper, for a few beers. I dragged a reporter colleague with me to show support for my buddy, Eddie Costa, who was on the program.

Other than working as a cashier at a local deli, he was a one-night, twice-a-year, very part-time comedian. It was his whole life.

"The Semi-Annual Special Olympics of Comedy," a purely commercial affair, was the featured event—open to handicapped persons with comedic acts capable of passing an audition, either good enough or bad enough to draw laughs. If the owners thought they had friends who might drop by, all the better. Even though I was the paper's unofficial expert in "special" matters by default, the comedy scene was a world I knew practically nothing about.

Knowing Eddie Costa was about it, which was almost worse than knowing nothing at all. But the guys around the block always tried to make the most of it for his sake.

A few of us would take him in a wheelchair into the City by subway and take him back, half in the bag, to his mother. That was pretty much it. However, the interpreter for the deaf was unbelievably hot, and the deaf comedian wasn't so bad herself.

Being a new-fangled journalist with a bloodlust for stories, I had to find out everything I could about these people—which was a good thing—because no one else did. Particularly my editor: "Nobody who reads this paper gives a shit about some dwarf telling dwarf jokes or a deaf guy telling a story with his hands to somebody who passes it on to everybody else."

Anyway, I talked him into letting me do a piece about the event; he didn't promise to print it. So, I poked around. I took notes about the night's events. Having no real hope for a featured story, maybe I could sell a full work-up or something substantial to the National Enquirer or The Sun.

That night, I put some personal sketches together, covered a few of the acts. I guess I got hooked on the thought of it. Of course, I already knew more about Eddie than I needed or wanted to.

With Eddie, it was all about him. If others engaged in combinations of id, ego, and superego to live in tortured harmony with themselves and fellow human beings, Eddie was one hundred percent ego, all the time, with nothing left for anyone else.

Being Eddie Costa was a full-time job.

Yet, he had more than his share of companions, advocates, and dear friends. And at the end of his life, even love—if that's what it was.

Edward Costa

Eddie occupied the low earth. Heavy gravity. Newtonian. Moving within God's geometry was a cruel injustice. He bent to it in twists of his head and swings of his legs and arms, riding his spine across streets and floors to gain scant headway in the invisible gale.

Thrust and tack.
Try to talk.
Tack again.
Try to breathe.

Even if he lurched around connected by strings to an unseen puppeteer, he was a person of limitless possibility. A person of unexpected laughs and insatiable needs.

In school, he was the class prankster, the one-of-a-kind handicapped kid with cerebral palsy who wound everybody up. He was the joker, the thrower of sounds and voices. He took Peggy McCartney, the prettiest girl in the neighborhood, to the prom. He wore a powder-blue tux and Peggy showed up in the prettiest dress she could afford. She danced with all the boys while Eddie fell three times, ruining the knees of his rented pants. They were the King and Queen of the Prom—Beauty and the Beast.

Rosaland Hernandez
Interpreter for the Deaf / Seer for the Blind
Eighth Street, New York, NY

It is the nature of light and sound to arrow in patterns through the air to the eye and ear, from transmitter to receiver, in wavelengths and currents through the senses in expected and unexpected signals and images to the brain.

Roz Hernandez moved in indifferent precision through this realm like a Hindu goddess with a dozen arms and tens of heads until a moment was achieved when it fused incarnate. She could sign the dance of a butterfly across a garden wall so a deaf girl

could hear its wings; she could speak so a blind man could see it
flutter.

She was the only Interpreter for the Deaf and Seer for the
Blind that the Komedy Klub, or anywhere else, ever had. She
would walk for the crippled and think for the simple-minded if
she could find a way. And someday, maybe she will.

Eugene Intartaglia

"When did you go blind?"
"When I took the gleam of Achilles' armor into
my eye on the plains of Ilium."
"Yes?"
"No, that was Homer. I was always blind."
"Is Homer your hero?"
"No. Polyphemus, the Cyclops, wasn't either. Not
Milton. Nor Oedipus the King."
"Who was?"

"My friend Louis who can draw what he can't see. Ray Charles.
Stevie Wonder. José Feliciano's dog and Galileo."
"Did Galileo look into his telescope after he lost his sight to 'see'
one more time the moons of Jupiter?"
"The stars come out to us only in the dark. For Galileo, the dark
was in the nature of the observer, not the nature of the stars to be
observed. The eye can't see, nor skin feel, and the ear don't hear.
It's all mind."
"What are you saying?"
"Just shitting with you."

Eugene came from the womb evolved to understand everything
he would ever know without sight. In rooms, on streets, moun-

taintops, and under the sky. This included blotches of light without edges that came from inside or from outside and both together. Whether fired from a dissolute optic nerve or a locomotive's headlights was all the same.

Sometimes, he would click like a bat or tap his cane to listen to the unseen contours around him to return echoes. An oven full of cupcakes smelled the shape of the kitchen. The chirping of crickets or a rumpus of kids playing in a lot filled his head with its boundaries. A breath of air had the shape of the tree it blew through. If he were a snake, he'd never stop flicking his tongue.

Even then, his perception was half-assed, fifty-fifty at best.

Lil' Sistah Coleman

The City was wheelchair-averse. Curbs were fortresses to mount even if you were accompanied. The streets were teeming with highways.

Heavy, wooden crutches dragged her everywhere. She swung over land on the sidewalks, up and down stairs, and through buildings in stages like a sea lion with crutches for flippers. She bumped downstairs one by one on her butt, holding her crutches across her chest. Her torso and arms were like a blacksmith's, shoulders like a lioness when she strode, her legs a ragdoll's.

Her name was Cicely Coleman, but everyone called her Lil' Sistah. Or Lil'. Lil'!

She lived in a New York City–run group home for the disabled downtown on the East Side and worked sitting down stuffing envelopes, fashioning wallets, key chains, and other solitary jobs—pure drudgery.

Not if you can sing!

And she sang like an angel if angels could sing. Sistah's situation gave her all day to sing a cappella. Sometimes at the shop *the workers sang together, taking turns picking songs to sing at the lead.*

Lil' Sistah was not intrinsically funny, yet she was invited to "The Comedy Special Olympics" at the KK twice a year. Who could blame her if she always went? She could sing a funny song as well as any other song. Watching and hearing her on a stage posted between her crutches, wearing a sailor's cap, rough sweater, jeans, and black sneakers, you'd be as likely to laugh as cry. Her specialty was Judy Garland. She was okay with The Supremes and anything Motown. Everyone was okay with Lil' Sistah.

The Ninety-Second Street Guys

With relatives, it was all DNA. At least you had some of you in there if they were losers. But who you grew up around in the neighborhood was random.

The nature of the guy next door had nothing to do with you. It's proximity—period. Who you play with, go to school with, and probably who you marry were all to do with adjacency and juxtaposition. We grew up on the same street—Ninety-Second Street—that was it.

No mean street either, unless those who didn't count were counted, those we tortured, played tricks on, and called names because we felt like it.
Midget Mary.
Crazy Mary and her kids.
Roller Blade Harry had no legs.
Parrot Mary lived in a shack in the lot next to the candy store with no electricity or water.

. . .

The Guys didn't so much care for each other, either, but became acculturated. And in time, Special Eddie Costa got to be one of the guys. Even if he could never keep up, was useless in a fight, had no ballgame skill, and had to be carted around pretty much everywhere, he was way smarter, meaner, and way funnier than us.

He was the vortex of attention, like sand in the eyeball of the neighborhood. He would fling pebbles from the curb during stickball games, spit toothpick bits on the table when we shot pool, or heckle anyone he felt like. He was master of abusing whatever sympathy came his way, master of making his life less miserable by making ours worse. After a while, we would miss him if he wasn't around.

The Komedy Klub
Eighth Street, New York, NY

The club was on an industrial side street on the Lower East Side of Manhattan between the high-rent apartments and upscale stores along Fifth Avenue and the run-down alphabet avenues off the East River. A barren of alleys and storefronts with hand-painted signs in Korean and Chinese and warehouses with metal trapdoors over storage basements that clanged half open when walked on. It was a dilapidated local stop on the Lexington Avenue Line. The KK.

Angled, sound-alike letters were cool for prescription drugs, corporate and product names. Exomazolyx was for loose bowels and DAT-A-BOYZ Q-Ball was a pool room. Qortni was somebody's sister.

The Fourth Semi-Annual
Special Olympics of Comedy, The KK
[December 18, 1972]

The bar intake was minimal. The handicapped trended toward sobriety, but the Komedy Klub made money on the cover charge coming in. It also drew regulars who appreciated the anger and goodness that seeped through the routines.

People said unexpected things when the joke was on them. Edward "Special Eddie" Costa was saved for the last act. Eugene—the Blind Guy; Sarah—the Sexy Deaf Woman; Lil' Sistah—the Crippled Lady; and Donatello—the Angry Midget were all on the card.

But Special Eddie was the star. At the end of the program, there was an "open mic" for disabled people who thought themselves humorists for as long as anyone was buying drinks.

Ray Hackett, Vinnie Di Paolo, and Jimmy Barbaro picked Eddie up at the apartment he shared with his mother in Brooklyn on Ninety-Second Street off Fort Hamilton Parkway, plopped him into the wheelchair he hated, and pushed him to the station on Ninety-Fifth.

Other friends from school and the neighborhood, including me, would meet them at the club. After a visit to the deli for a six-pack they drank and dumped in trash cans along the way, they took turns riding the back of Eddie's wheelchair. Bumped down the stairs to the edge of the tracks while he closed his eyes to his opening remarks. Forty minutes later, the guys were doing wheelies with Eddie up Eighth Street in the East Village.

Roz Hernandez nurtured the crowd, signing for the deaf and commenting to the blind through the opening acts. She was long, thin, and serene, in her early twenties with pushed-back, lark-black hair that undid with the evening. But it was her Giacometti legs and arms that enthralled, amplified with shining bracelets, multicolored blouses with flowing sleeves, and tight rah-rah skirts. Unpleasant or mundane statements would flow through her in American Sign Language like ballet or kabuki. She would sign I want to vomit, and men wanted to sleep with her. She told the blind how tears gathered in a comedian's eyes, or said, "The lights are turning purple, dimming," while signing to the deaf what a performer said. Men tried to buy her drinks or set up dates after hours to no avail.

She was Roz.

Eugene's View
9:30 p.m.

After forty-five minutes of jokes by people with obvious disorders and a session of midget gags that caught the absurdity of their lives a lot better than the grace, there was a weepy, beautiful song played on a badly tuned piano by Eugene Tartaglia that included a slender, ad-lib monologue he delivered throughout, about the imagine-world of the blind and the unseeable KK world around him. Roz did what she could do.

He played and sang "I'll Be Seeing You."
I'll be seeing you,
In all the old familiar places,
That this heart of mine embraces,
All day through.

"There is a large open space over there, that fills with confusion and coldness," – Eugene.

"Yes, Eugene. Lobby near door," – Roz.

In that small café,
The park across the way,
The children's carousel,
The chestnut trees, the wishing well.

"And in front right, tables of chaos, of course, but not to them.
Like orphans at the Christmas Dinner." – E.

I'll be seeing you in every lovely summer's day and,
Everything that's light and gay,
I'll always think of you that way,
I'll find you in the morning sun.

"The deaf are there, Eugene. Eugene?
Do you rock your head when you play?" – R.

"If I could see the keys,
would I rock my eyes to sample the air?
Would I roll to hear the chamber where
the hammers strike the strings to sing?" – E.

I will find you in the morning sun and,
When the night is new,
I'll be looking at the moon,
While I'll be seeing you.

"I can't see the color of the walls, but they're dark. Wheelchairs are there. And it's stumpy for a stage room like this. A
little higher than a tall person. With a sign printed 'Komedy
Klub' over my head." – E.

And when the night is new,
I'll be looking at the moon,

But I'll be seeing you.

"Yes, Eugene. How did you know?" – R.

      "Sounds go quickly in open space. Tables with tablecloths and chairs with people get in the way. Other reasons. Cigarette smells echo and bounce around. People smell. Got to be a KK sign somewheres. Right?" – E.

"Yes, Eugene." – R.
A man stood to say,
"How tall am I, Eugene?"
"Small." – E.
"How small, Eugene?" – R.
"Very." – E.
"Yes." – R.

Yes, I'll be seeing you in every lovely summer's day,
And everything that's light and gay,
I'll always think of you that way.

"How tall is my friend here?" the guy asked.
"Yeah. How tall am I?"
"No more than average height." – E.

I will find you in the morning sun and,
When the night is new,
I'll be looking at the moon,
But I'll be seeing you.

"Yes, Eugene. He's standing on a chair." – R.

Yes, I will find you in the early bright and

When the night is new
I'll be looking at the moon
But I'll be seeing you.

"He'll get down." – E.

People clapped. The piano was rolled away.

Sarah Stanley
9:55 p.m.

Sarah ran on stage to deaf cheers and loud applause. She signed the love sign to the audience: three fingers—thumb, index, pinky out—then pressed palms together with Roz on stage. Roz told the blind what they could not see, "*Sarah gorgeous in red-hot dress. Cleavage when breathes.*"

Sarah signed and Roz translated. It was unclear whether Roz's translations preceded Sarah's signs, even though that was improbable.

"*You know, the deaf had a very special Special Olympics Debating Team. Everything went well until we took on Team Blind.*"

The blind bobbed their heads and spoke to the air in front of them in their taciturn, alert way, with little cheers and tapping canes. Unlike almost everyone else, they didn't smoke. What was the point of blowing smoke into the air if it could not be seen and tasted like burnt shit?

Alone in their private darknesses, they laughed more inwardly, their dogs harrumphing into on-duty snoozes.

The deaf stuck together, ignored the performers except their own, drank too much out of beer pitchers, smoked too much, signed too loudly—if that could be said—with grunts and smacks for attention. Paced to the rhythms between them, Sarah's signs were Roz's words and vice versa.

They were best friends.

"None on our team heard, naturally, what the debate question was. We went with the old standard, the Death Penalty. We took both sides to be safe. While we fucked up the whole point, our presentation was so strong, our signing so fast and so passionately passionate—the scorers had no idea what we were signing—so we got the highest score possible, 10 out of 10 for presentation but zero for content.

"The topic was Proportional Representation in the Senate, which of course the blind team nailed 10 out of 10, but one girl tripped on an electrical cord and pulled down the podium sending notes and service dogs flying. They got no points for presentation and zip for visual effects; they didn't have any.

"Both teams were so very Special, we were disqualified."

Sarah was perspiring through her dress and wouldn't sit for the next thirty minutes. "Last week I went for a car ride with my friends. Ever ride with a deaf driver?"

The deaf tables slapped each other while Sarah played all the roles: the deaf driver and passenger, and a hearing person pointing and screaming from the back seat. Her stool was her car. The audience thought the idea amusing, while Sarah and Roz worked at double speed to make it work.

It was approaching 10:30 p.m. Sarah finished sampling the deaf comedy canon. How being deaf was better than anything else. She was right.

Sarah leaped into her friends' arms as the MC took the microphone.

Lil' Sistah's Song

10:35 p.m.

The announcer shouted, "Sistahahahah!" She dragged herself across the stage on wooden crutches which thumped notwithstanding rubber tips. She thought it was multiple sclerosis. Maybe it was.

She said "Hi" so oddly into the mic it caused a nasty feedback screech, making her crumble her head into her shoulders.

Those that could, answered, "Hi, Sis."

Those who couldn't waved with open palms next to their heads.

People in wheelchairs lined up in designated areas like at a ball game or church service. They made do with the people next to them, drank amateurish drinks in luminous colors stuck in cup holders to their wheelchairs: Arctic Kiss, Vampire Juice, Purple Hemorrhage.

Caregivers hung at the bar getting high among black-and-white photos of dead comedians taken when it was Tony's Comedy Central: The Great Gildersleeve, Fred Allen, Red Skelton, and Nipsey Russell.

She wore her everyday workshop outfit—jeans, pullover, and blue sailor's cap. She would have worn a cute little dress with frilly white socks for her song tonight if she didn't have to take the No. 6 subway to the club, which required bumping down icy, filthy steps holding her crutches to her chest down the Twenty-Eighth Street Station stairs to take the local train to Bleecker Street, where she performed the near-impossible reverse climb up the stairs back into the street.

There, she dragged her legs behind her crutches to the Komedy Klub. Someone opened the door for her when she knocked to flop on the nearest open chair to exchange her black sneakers for red patent-leather shoes she carried in a backpack.

After her song, everyone will be smiling because of the way she will sing it—straight and a cappella—with the audience signing or singing along with Munchkins unseen, and it will be ironic and sad if not exactly funny. But everyone will have a certain amount of love for Lil' Sistah, pegging across the stage and marching in circles:

Follow the Yellow Brick Road.
Follow the Yellow Brick Road.
Follow, follow, follow, follow.
Follow the rainbow over the stream,
Follow the fella who follows a dream,
follow, follow, follow,
Follow, follow the yellow brick road.

Sistah stumped and skipped around the floor holding the mic on the crutch handle. A red ribbon had been planted on her sailor's cap. Her body was dense and stubborn, but her voice tender, optimistic. And she didn't ham it up or try to add to the irony.

She tried to be Dorothy.

Toward the end of the routine, Special Eddie Costa joined her on stage, something he had never done before—nor could he skip, no matter how he tried. But Lil' Sistah had never sung "Follow the Yellow Brick Road" before either, and Eddie was by nature the Lion, Scarecrow, and Tin Man each together and severally.

They danced across the stage—Eddie tilting backward; Sistah tilting forward, crutch to crutch. They held hands when they could in unintended ways.

"We're off to see the Wizard,
the Wonderful Wizard of Oz.

*We'll find he is a Whiz of a Wiz
If ever a Wiz there was."*

The middle aisle soon filled with those mobile enough to skip—or close enough.

*"If ever oh ever a Wiz there was,
The Wizard of Oz is one because,
Because, because, because, becaauuuuse . . .
because of the wonderful things he does.
We're off to see the Wizard.
The Wonderful Wizard of Oz."*

Roz became a light tower in the middle of the stage to shine the rhythms and lyrics around the room to the blind and the deaf.

In twenty minutes, Little Sistah's tour around the yellow brick road was over. Special Eddie sat exhausted on the edge of the stage. He was up next. Sis changed into her sneakers and went home unnoticed. She thumped slowly the mile and three-quarters to her room at the shelter, not wanting to hack another trip down and up the subway stairs nor waste the fifteen cents. The Americans with Disabilities Act was twenty years away.

She sang every song of the Judy Garland songbook up Seventh Avenue to Avenue A. Anyway, that's what they say.

*Merry Little Christmas
The Trolley Song
Meet Me in St. Louis, Louis
Come On Get Happy*

She was concluding "Over the Rainbow" as she neared East

Tenth Street. If so, she must have planned it. Perhaps it was an urban legend.

Special Eddie. Spotlight
10:55 p.m.

"Ladies, Gentlemen, and Special Guests, what you've all been waiting for, Edward 'Special Eddie' Costa!"

Eddie's act was what was left of his life. The spotlight found him fighting to get out of his chair. Those who could whistle, whistled. Vinnie Di Paolo smacked him on the back of his head and people threw balled-up napkins as Eddie edged, crabwise, to walk.

At centerstage was a stool and a microphone. If he kept the mic on its stand, he had no hope to center it to his mouth, which moved always and unpredictably with his head. If he held it, he had a chance to sync up the constant rock and sway. So, he held the stand with his left hand for balance, waved the loose mic in his more spastic right hand, and rolled his head to the beat of the room and the random course of the microphone.

He liked the look and feel. A circus tiger pawing on a stool.

This was Special Eddie's fourth semi-annual Special Olympics of Comedy.

What he told them wasn't as important as what he didn't. He didn't tell them how special they were. They knew.

Special Eddie leaned against his stool. Outside the street was quiet, except for occasional thumps from trucks unseating manhole covers. Something he was not in charge of—a wince or a shudder—crossed Eddie's face in lieu of a smile. He went with pretending that everything his face and body did was on purpose. People laughed.

"So, my mother is waiting to see her new little darling Edward in the hospital."

While his head took its tilts and trips, his voice settled and tuned. Still, it took twice as long as normal speech, like a mechanical voice box, to reach the world. Eddie's words, like Sarah's, took time.

Words spoken through Sarah's hands retold by her interpreter lagged seconds between them. Eddie's words nudged through hardened organs and the separate conveyors of speech: larynx, lungs, trachea, vocal folds. Whether French, German, English, or Chinese, each CP speaker spoke the language of cerebral palsy. Each syllable a word, each phrase stitched within each sentence fought to squeeze its way out.

"The nurse brings me in after putting Mom off for as long as possible. 'He's in the laundry,' she says.

'He's been sent to the boiler room,' she says.

Finally, she says, 'Oh, here he is now!' My mother peeks under the blanket, 'Oh, how adorable. A platypus!'"

Eddie turned his sideways face to the laughter, which Roz described to the blind as a "Jack Benny pout."

Most of his intro was reinterpreted, set pieces. If he did too much new material, people complained or asked for certain riffs:

"Eddie, tell us about when you got drunk in high school."

"Do your first date routine."

"What about LBJ's retarded brother?"

Eddie cribbed jokes from books and late-night TV he twisted to fit himself. He continued along the lines of Baby Edward for minutes.

"The nurse insisted, 'No, no. Mrs. Costa, it's your little Edward.'

Mom said, 'Yeah? Which end gets the diapers?'"

"This is my fourth Stand-Up Special Olympics at the KK," he said, backing onto the stool. He was used to chairs, wheelchairs, immobility—but he was never still. The mic looped in front of his mouth. So far, so good.

He wore a suit popular in the jazz era. Macy's didn't have a cerebral palsy department. He made do with what was around from his dead father.

Eddie used to wear sweeping-necked, shiny silk shirts that opened to the middle button with pointed bat-wing collars and gold-looking, swinging pendants around his neck. Male singers and dancers used these outfits for a decade with tight bell-bottomed pants, leatherette boots, and sequined jumpsuits without waists.

These outfits, Eddie believed, made him a star. He'd drag them out when his mother was at work for angles and poses in the mirror, but they were costly—people said snide things, and rather than make him look like Elvis, they made him look like a guy with cerebral palsy in an Elvis suit.

Tonight, it was a wide-shouldered, black, double-breasted, pinstriped zoot suit, a purple silk shirt, and no tie.

"I tried out for the real Special Olympics last year," he said.

"They said I was so special I was overqualified."

A chuckle passed.

"But they put me on the Cerebral Palsy Team to play the Down's Team in basketball to a four-hour, zero-zero tie. The Downs guys could dribble the ball but didn't know what they were doing, and the CP folks knew what we were doing, but couldn't dribble. We could barely walk. The not-so-good dribbling was mixed with a lot of great drooling. It was hard to watch; it turned out no one was."

Eddie sat lower on the stool to pooch under smoke twisting in convection currents just over his head. He picked a cigarette with practiced but authentic difficulty out of a Camel soft pack with his lips.

After a couple of tap-taps with his better hand on the stool —very professional—he tried to light it. He worked the click of the lid, the rasp of the flint wheel, and the sudden flame-up. The fire chased the cigarette around until he used his mic-holding hand to steady his face.

He smoked on stage for effect, flicking ashes on himself, finding and missing his mouth, half on purpose—not really. What wasn't planned he played for its Special Eddie-ness.

The room was on-and-off bright or ghostly dark as the combo bouncer–lighting man applied mood changes with yellow to purple-red filters that dyed the smoke layers and the performers.

The walls were painted black, the bricks behind the stage, black; black plastic covered the tables; the waiters and bartenders wore black. The stool was dark purple. Eddie had a dark purple stool just like it in his apartment, grooved by his feet to the bare wood along the rails. He practiced moves and looks in the living room mirror. How to light a cigarette and make the Fuck You stare so it might be a joke—or not. He recaptured mistakes and worked on personal tics that made people laugh.

He was the star of the mirror, telling jokes and anecdotes over the sounds of the traffic and the kids playing on Ninety-Second Street. He worked on the effects he wanted—the disabled man with a microphone in his hand, pitiful, pathetic— but don't count on it. There was danger behind the underdog smirk. He practiced the look that said he might leap off the stool to stick his nails into your eyeballs, or fly like a bat in the middle of a set out the window into the city night.

He practiced all this, as well as moving his mouth and head in rhythm with a wooden spoon for a mic, while his mother was at work. His mother hated Eddie's routine, so he rehearsed when his mother was out, or silently when she was in her room. He never made fun of his mother.

The tables of deaf men and women continued to sign private conversations. Glasses clanked, plates fell, people fell, jackets came off and went on with grunts and gestures. Everything was large and loud on the deaf side of life tonight.

"Hey! Youze over there. I'm trying to conduct a church service here," Eddie said.

Roz signed the "youze," including the z.

"Hey, screw yourself!" somebody at the offending table signed in reply to Eddie, which Roz translated. Eddie fell back at the words.

"Roz! You stay out of this. I'm trying to communicate to this baboon over here."

Whenever he could fit it in, he blamed Roz for the signs she interpreted. It was part of his bit. Their bit.

The deaf guy was also mock-hurt and collapsed into his chair as Eddie began a longish gag about the "Special" joys associated with romantic dancing between a man with cerebral palsy and a deaf woman. Eddie hummed into the microphone and signed fake American Sign Language sequences—many obscene—at the offending table and his fantasy partner while duck-walking cha-cha moves around the stool.

Tall, adagio, Roz signed what was said and spoke what needed to be seen, like shuffling decks of cards from hand to hand in the air in mock sophistication.

When he finished, Eddie gathered himself on the stool with Roz nearby.

"Heavy breathing. Heavy heart beating," she said.

Special Eddie checked out the people at the tables and in the wheelchairs. The with-it guys at the bar spun their chairs toward the stage. The deaf returned from each other to watch Eddie's next move. Even the bartenders stopped washing glasses and preparing drinks. The lighting–bouncer guy adjusted the lights to the new dispensation, deep blue for Eddie tonight. His head craned against his neck.

It was Eddie's time.

Somebody shouted, "Tell us about it, Eddie!"

"You wanna know about it? I'll tell you about it."

He put his cigarette out, but it already was.

Eddie's Harangue

11:47 p.m.

Every Special Eddie performance had its rant. Whether it was planned or impromptu wasn't always clear. Except maybe to Roz.

She was never surprised by anything he did or said. His exact outburst may have been unknown, but it was always some form of retaliation for how his life sucked or someone else's life like his sucked. Or how everybody's life did. These people weren't the children running around the tracks at Special Olympics events or happy to be stuffing envelopes at the Home for the Handicapped.

Eddie's people were aggrieved; sometimes they blamed God or fate or bad luck for their bad luck, maybe themselves or humankind generally, but they knew they had nothing to feel special about—unless it was special bad. Twice a year, they let Eddie "tell them about it."

"They say we're Special. Special to be disabled or otherwise inappropriate. But in heaven . . . in heaven, God's going to make it up for giving us such shitty lives. A tough break. Because we're so Special. There's nothing better than people feeling sorry by giving us stuff to do, which we really can't. Like run around the track at zero-point-zero miles an hour, jump hurdles, or play with bowling balls. Or me, telling jokes sounding like I'm underwater."

Eddie wasn't looking so great. Or he was faking. Nobody could tell.

Jimmy Barbaro wanted to wrap Eddie in a cape, help him offstage to make a comeback like Eddie's rhythm-and-blues hero, James Brown, but Eddie didn't like to be touched.

"It's not like it's not appreciated. I just weigh what I get against what I got, and it ain't enough. Thank you, but I live a miserable life. How about you?"

Those who could stand stood or cheered from wheelchairs or yelled in place. Service dogs politely smelled the air and the deaf pumped their fists in front of their chests.

"And Heaven? Us? Me? Schlepping around heaven bent sideways. Or you. You're in a wheelchair and have to get some guy you don't know lift you under your armpits to stretch the pain and cramps out of your back bones like you're a rag to wring. Or you're walking your head into walls trying to learn to use a cane for eyes. Or are half run over by a truck that's blowing its horn, but you and your friend are signing a joke to each other in ASL—ha, ha—but there's no ASL sign a truck makes for a horn—nor squealing tires.

"No tree signs the sound the wind makes through its leaves. Nor the sound of your lover's heartbeat you feel but you'll never hear. But. But you feel the breeze in your hair and your lover's blood against yours. You better make it work in your own heaven. Thanks very much but you ain't going near theirs."

"So, Joe, a guy with cerebral palsy, is lucky enough to die in his sleep. He knows he's dead because his head's on right, his legs don't cramp, and his bones don't cross."

"He tries to wake up one of St. Peter's secretaries who is dozing at his desk. There's a sign: The Blessed Bruce, Under Secretary of SPECIAL Affairs, Security & Quality Control Division. Joe gives a poke, 'Excuse me. Bruce? It's me, Joe.'"

"Bruce rubs his eyes, then right away feels sorry for Joe after checking him out. He says, 'Listen, Bub, I'll talk to the Man. Let's see your rap sheet.'

"Bruce has about a thousand millennia to his next promotion, so he takes his time going through the books, planetary divisions, and consciousness matrixes. It's a big universe. Joe's records are in Aramaic, so Bruce has to make a few phone calls. The result: Joe swore a couple'a times. Once, he kicked a cat. What kind of sins is this guy gonna commit? Rob a stagecoach?"

Eddie waved an imaginary gun in his spastic hand like a child's rattle. "Ah, stand and deliver. It's a stick-up!" he said like Bugs Bunny.

"What, he cheats on his wife? What wife? I wanted to get married once. So, I talk to the girl's father. I say, 'I'd like to marry your daughter.'

"He says, 'What!? It's a girl?'

"I say, 'She's not? I mean, he's not?'

"The guy says, 'How the fuck do I know?'

"So, I say to him before I take home whatever, 'Did she come with instructions?' He kicked me out. I left alone and bought a turtle."

He made us wait again as he lip-clipped another cigarette out of the crumbled pack he shared with the stool. His mother wouldn't let him smoke in the apartment. He looked like he enjoyed the release when it came out under the lights.

"Purple-blue smoke-stream is in the room," Roz said. He spat a tobacco bit, if he was lucky.

"So, Bruce says, 'Joe. Go right into Heaven. I don't think sinning was your forte.'

"So, in Joe goes, all smiles, tries to walk tall and strut proud. 'I'll just mosey along right on into Heaven.'"

Eddie staggered an exaggerated palsy-walk around the stool, dumpty dumpty-dum, like it was a Maypole, beaming angelically, moving on up through Heaven's Gate where he belongs. "'Next stop Infinity, baby!'"

"Meanwhile, St. Peter is rolling a joint behind a cloud and something catches his eye. It's Mr. Joe sliding along, singing a song. St. Pete says, 'What the frig's that!? Whoa, Dude! Where you goin'?'"

Eddie was back on the stool, looked around, took a drag, but the cigarette was out. He flicked it at Roz, who ducked.

"Do you honestly think they want us hanging around to bum them out—all the saints—us bumping into them with our guide dogs and canes, 'Oh. Excuse me, Mr. St. Francis. Didn't mean to interrupt.' Falling down, blubbering around heaven in front of Mother Flippin' Teresa and the philanthropists with initials between their names on hospital wings?"

Folks clapped along, like it was a long talking-blues riff they'd heard before. He spoke into the noise and the beat.

"Sure, they won't mind stepping over you having a seizure on the ground and your catatonic stares, white foam stuck to the hinges of your mouth, or your paranoid visions of every level of Hell on Earth in Heaven. No no. Surely not the Murdered Martyrs and Goody-Goodies and the Righteous Right, them that got Born Again like it says in the Bible, Hallelujah!

"The collected-together Fathers and the collected virtuous Mothers dressed in their Sunday Heaven outfits?

"The Bible thumpers and the old Greaseball Popes floating together among the clouds? All the Bleeding Heart, Good Samaritan, Humanitarian, Well-Intended, High-Minded, Parlor Deacons and the Rocking Chair Jesuses?

"Your Fairy Godparents are playing harps in Heaven and Santy Claus is talking to a couple'a Archangels about the Christmas pageant. Where do YOU fit in?

"A guy with a permanent stigmata is bleeding sweet blood 'round heaven all day and now YOU die of leprosy with your nose falling off, or have Down's or can't see or talk or hear, or you got encephalitis, or everything about you don't work right and never did. You think you're coming when you're going. What do YOU think?

"I've got news. YOU ain't going nor coming into no frigin' Heaven."

He didn't have much left.

"Roz, you're signing with a Puerto Rican accent again. It's confusing everybody."

She signed the laughter and told the blind how red and wired Eddie's eyes were, how short his breaths were breathing.

Roz rocked and Roz rolled with her hands over her head, seven feet tall with goddess arms like entwinning snakes. She shaped Eddie's words, and she told the blind what to see, and when she was finished, the anger and the laughter were gone. Even what was funny wasn't funny anymore.

Special Eddie placed the mic on the stool. Roz helped him offstage to a mix of applause and nothing.

This was what Special Eddie lived for. He'd have to rethink it, remix it for greatness, errors, opportunities missed for the next six months while dragging himself down the stairs to the grocery store to get some air, smoke some, and stretch his twisted self. Rethink it for the next time. What to say and what to do. But there will be no next time.

This was Special Eddie's last Special Olympics of Comedy. People disappear into the City all the time. Maybe he was absorbed into the night or fell into Special Heaven or Hell.

Eddie wasn't there when the guys looked to take him home. Perhaps he was curled against a curb or through the tired night into the Bronx or Queens. His wheelchair was gone. No one saw him leave. Jimmy Barbaro called the cops.

At 2 a.m., he called Mrs. Costa—go to sleep, not to worry, Eddie was a big hit. He gave her plausible lies she didn't believe. We rode the subways in three directions until dawn.

The police phoned Mrs. Costa in the morning to tell her that scores of "persons" go missing every night. They would put Edward's description into the system, check the Transit Authority, the hospitals. And the morgue—but they didn't say that to Mrs. Costa.

Two days into Eddie's disappearance, I was informed by friends at the 69th Precinct that Roz Hernandez had been unaccounted for since Thursday, when she didn't show for her job at Hamilton High School. The cops were nice enough to keep me apprised if anything turned up, which didn't.

We told Mrs. Costa that Eddie was off with a woman from the KK. She was reconciled to thinking he was at least alive. But Eddie with a woman?

A month later, a card with a Harrisburg, Pennsylvania postmark arrived addressed to Mrs. Costa. "Sorry Mom. I'm okay. I'm with a friend. Try to forget I ever existed. Love, Edward."

That was exactly what she had been doing.

What was known about Eddie and Roz's cross-country excursion I pieced together on a fact-finding journey several months later. Why I did this I don't know. I have a compulsive side.

I suspected there wasn't a "story" there, except maybe a tearjerker or one of those real-life dramas people would rather not read and didn't.

I had a seven-day vacation owed me from the paper, so I hit the road—but not before calling all the comedy joints within 200 miles. Taking off without warning was clearly in Eddie's psychotic toolbox. None of the guys around the neighborhood nor his mother had a clue beyond that. Obviously, it wouldn't take more than Roz's presence to get Eddie to hit the road. Roz's motives were more mysterious.

I reckoned for Roz it was more an adventure out of creative boredom or laxity of spirit, certainly no romantic escapade. A better guess would be it had to do with inventing a life beyond the "handicapped" crowd. To initiate, not interpret. To be the star she was.

Brody's Roadhouse
Carlisle, PA

Eddie had never been on a road trip, had never been out of Brooklyn except to take the subway with his mother or travel with the guys to a game at the Garden, screw around outside the dirty movies and porn shops a bit, or go to a KK gig twice a year.

The wide world now came at him for the first time through a windshield. Sit back. Relax with Roz at the wheel to watch mountaintops in the distance brighten in the morning sun, to see fields and trees blur by as scattered farmhouses fell into lazy streets in towns, and country roads roamed the foothills and valleys.

Their first gig was Brody's Roadhouse. Judging from how they were remembered, Roz and Eddie did straight comedy sketches and improvised scenes they coordinated to smooth his off-kilter ways of walking, talking, and inability to be still for more than a moment.

Things that disabled audiences would laugh at were not humorous to the average Midwesterner. Yet, their "Beauty and the Beast" appeal did count for something. Eddie was nothing if not quick on his feet, even if they were splayed and his delivery took forever.

The biggest experiment, however, was Roz's ascent to speak her words, move her moves, shine her shine. Their collected oddness could hold an audience's attention, but it would take Roz's Rozness to capture them. I knew Eddie had zero money, even for food. They must have emptied her bank account. They stayed in Motel 6s traveling west.

Columbus, Dayton, Fort Wayne,
Terre Haute, and Paducah
October through January

After a while, they scuttled the motels to stay for periods through Ohio and Indiana at cheap rooming houses to hone the rough edges before gigs. Running out of cash, and with nothing much happening, they needed help.

Roz made the call.

Sarah Stanley joined them in Terre Haute, Indiana. It had to be done. Even if it meant bringing American Sign Language back into Roz's life. Yet her signing was worth the price of admission to those who could appreciate the music of her body in motion. Sarah's presence also brought physical comedy into the act. She was nothing if not visual.

Apparently, Roz and Sarah were close. Eddie was not happy. He was never happy. Sarah opened skits of unexpected moments. With Eddie as foil, the act improvised through Indiana and Kentucky. In one skit, Eddie confused Roz's translations of Sarah's come-on remarks as invitations for unlikely threesomes. Clearly ridiculous. People laughed. The trio took bows. They were getting better.

The big hit was Sarah's car routine from the KK. Two distracted deaf people, including the driver, sign to each other in a happy frenzy in the front seat while ignoring the road. With three chairs for props, Eddie yelled from the back, pointing at potential dangers on the road.

It worked best when Eddie used the audience as road obstacles and unexpected perils. But what worked best was a surprising song, "Among the Moons of Saturn," about a colony of mentally, physically, cosmologically disabled people, and KK Special Olympic comrades, who rollicked around Saturn doing what they do there—screw around and make love in the moony weightless spaces at the edges of the solar system. The trio appeared to enjoy themselves as much as the audience.

The full array of "Special" unfortunates became Saturn's new royalty, fornicating in Dionysian circles in the phosphorus glare. It was nearly perfect. Except—they couldn't sing. There were only two voices, and Eddie didn't really have a voice.

Roz made the call.

Elfin, lame Lil' Sistah joined them in Des Moines.

It must have been hellish for three young women with a carload of luggage, including Eddie's spider-presence, not to mention sleeping arrangements in double-bed motel rooms.

Lil' couldn't play an instrument, but she sure could sing.

Wooly's Outpost
Des Moines, Iowa
[January 1973]

One Wooly's Outpost witness recalled that the Moons began their Sexy Outer Space Blues Hymn to the Handicapped in discordant joy:

"Introducing the cosmic comedy of 'The Moons of Saturn!'"
the MC said.

Oh, the Leonids are yearly in Leo,
And Halley's is flyin' o'er Orion,
But the crips and the limbless
Float ever-ry night
In Titan's heavenly glow.

. . . .
And so forth.

No one noticed that the words changed nightly. It was all noise and as corny as that. Roz slapped at an acoustic guitar hung bongo-style. Eddie made noise with a clarinet.

Sarah breathed in and out of a Dylanesque face-harpoon that left her hands free to spin signs in solipsistic inattention. But over everything, Lil' Sistah's voice rang, crutches thumping in timed tattoo: bump – pa-bump – pa-bump-bump-bump. They played for three nights in Des Moines. By the last performance, Lil' Sistah begged them—if they ever got back to New York—to get Eugene the blind guy on piano.

If the beat and material were off-putting, no one from Iowa had been to Saturn, either, so shut up. This was no Lower East

Side Komedy Klub routine, nor twangy country-blues riff. This was Saturn, baby!

Heisenberg meets Ray Charles.

I left the trail in Iowa. My editor beckoned with an assignment. I drove from the Midwest to Brooklyn in a day and a half to cover the Norwegian Day Parade along Third Avenue in Bay Ridge—a big deal in the neighborhood if you were Norwegian. I wasn't, but I got to take a real photographer with me for the first time.

A month later, Mickey Lafferty got a call from a former girlfriend who moved to Florida about a handicapped comedy/song act from NYC called "The Moons of Something" appearing at the Something-House in Fort Myers. They said they were headed home: "To New York City." What?!

None of us had been to the KK for over a year, but that March the club's combo bouncer–lighting man passed word around town to watch The American Lampoon Comedy Hour, an edgy program of skits performed ensemble-style Sunday nights at 10 p.m.

"You're in for a Special treat," he said. Wednesday, Jimmy Barbaro got a call from Eddie. The Lampoon people put the Moons up in the Chelsea Hotel for a nip at the Big Apple. Sarah's car bit, which was now nearly perfect—with Roz next to her in the front seat, Eddie and Lil' flipping out behind them, and "Eugene and his dog Ralph doing God knows?"

I called Eddie at the hotel two days before the show.

"You piece of shit," I said.

"What do you expect? I'm not normal. You know that."

"I hope you called your mother. I admit she's been doing fine, far as we can tell. She showed us your postcard. You piece of shit."

"I called her when we arrived. She sounded disappointed."

"Do you blame her? Why didn't you call or let us in on it. What were you thinking?"

"What makes you think I was thinking? Whether I died or lived was of no particular interest, until Roz, but now I have no idea. I just keep moving."

I hung up.

Mulcahy's Bar & Grill
Sunday Evening
[October 12, 1973]

The corps of Eddie's drinking buds not already deployed somewhere "in country" in Southeast Asia—principally Dolan, Di Paolo, Billy Olsen, Barbaro, and I—set up under Mr. Mulcahy's 18-inch Philco TV leering at us over the bar. We had been there since 7 p.m. and promised to relinquish the television if it wasn't Eddie, so the old Donkeys, Polacks, and Squareheads didn't have shit fits with their Sunday ties pulled down around their sixth or seventh beer and balls with Mannix on at 11 p.m.

The gang and I were half in the bag ourselves, including Billy Olsen's girlfriend Gabriella, who thought I was Lafferty, who wasn't there. She was wearing a floppy Amish lady's bonnet and a sixteenth-century tavern wench outfit with puffy, Snow-White sleeves. Just like her. Too easy to take advantage of on Mickey's ticket. Plus, I was technically on the job.

At ten o'clock we turned the television on. Work-up music played over the American Lampoon logo while a sandy-voiced announcer dude drew out:

"L-i-v-e from New York! It's The American Lampoon Comedy Hour!"

As opening credits scrolled, the Moons did their "Among the Moons of Saturn" song. The camera shifted into a rolling scan of the troupe at their instruments.

Lil' Sistah held a long soprano note as the song wrapped into a swirling orgy under the soupy skies of Phoebe. They yielded to commercials and a skit by the regular American Lampoon crew about a tattoo parlor and secret rooms in the basement of a Washington, D.C. Senate Office Building. We asked Mr. Mulcahy if there were any specials.

The "Grilled Cheese Special" was special, as it had been since the arrival of the cheese five months earlier. We squeezed in another round as the cheese sizzled and hurried back to our spot by the TV. Gabriella flowed anon. I made her model it. I confessed I wasn't Lafferty. She did not ask who I was.

The announcer: "Introducing the cosmic comedy of 'The Moons of Saturn!'"

I took notes: *Roz and Sarah are teaching Eddie and Lil' Sistah American Sign Language so "everyone gets along." Easy at first, but ensuing double entendres and crude misunderstandings soon arose that Eddie and Lil' acted out to comic effect upon each other.*

It was oddly zany, different at least. Two American Lampoon skits by the regulars later, and as the Moons were readying the four chairs for Sarah's surefire car routine, the director indicated through the announcer that "time has run out for this week's show, but will 'The Moons of Saturn' join us for another skit on next week's show? How a-bout it?"

Try to stop them.

The Chelsea Hotel
[March 14–18, 1973]

Then everything changed.

First, the Lampoon's legal people insisted the Moons pre-record the car skit live to avoid lawsuits with handicapped people performing a live routine potentially poking each other's eyes out and falling off chairs for car seats. Add Eugene and his dog—no way. Plus, they could rent a real car that wouldn't have to leave the parking lot.

I called Eddie at the hotel to find him over the moon about the new setup, which he saw as "a big-time production" with five characters and a dog, cinema verité and essentially script-less with "roles up in the air." Eddie heaven.

The only reason the Moons needed to be in studio on Sunday night was for the "Goodbye Mingle" and for the cast party after. It would be hard to keep Eddie sober and nearly impossible to keep Lil' Sistah clean that long, but both were up for it and Roz told the AL staff she'd "personally" make it happen. That's the way she was.

Mulcahy's
Next Sunday Night

The bar was packed with neighborhood and high school friends, dates, spouses, and locals in their twenties. A few old men knotted together as far away from the TV as possible.

There was a 30-minute wait for the "Grilled Cheese Special" and the only toilet backed up onto the floor an hour before showtime. Weed was in the air.

The bar cat with no name, who would normally be taking his chances with selected customers, tried to sleep in the basement. In this atmosphere, it was possible for the world inside Mulcahy's to become suddenly unusual. It was as if you just started digesting how weird it all was, when next to you a girl with the same look in her eye was about to grab your hand and head for the nearest cliff.

A guy you called Georgie distributed peyote tea without asking, some of which was mixed into my beer as a present. Otherwise, I was fine.

American Lampoon intro music gravitated everyone to the TV screen. There were cheers and jockeying around as the new, improved, "Among the Moons" song played, taped among a celestial backdrop. At any moment, the Moons' video would start.

At 10:30 p.m., the MC crowed:

"The Ride Home from the Club – The Moons of Saturn." I went near the pool table to take half-concealed notes in relative peace.

The impossibility of being seriously undercover was secretly cool. To be and be not. On screen, the tape began: Roz and Sarah talk sign images to each other at dawn on a sidewalk adjacent to a Brooklyn warehouse that doubles as an after-hours joint. As the sun peaks over Long Island, Ralph, the dog, pulls Eugene to a fire hydrant. Roz goes for her keys to take the gang home, drops them. She looks like she could do with a whiz herself. "Whoops."

Sarah tries to help, tumbles over, signs "Whoops" with a swipe across her face.

They crawl along the sidewalk, laughing, signing Drunk American Sign Language (DASL), trying to find her keys.

Sarah signs the "drunk" sign with both hands shaking loosely in front of her face.

Roz finds the keys, tries unsuccessfully to stand, drops them, "Whoops." The streets are empty. Eugene holds his spot on the sidewalk in the sun, warming in the dawn's early light, offers: "We can crash at my place. If we can find it. Sarah knows the way." Eddie shambles forward as if to speak. Eugene anticipates hearing what he does not want to hear:

"Eugene, I'll walk you to the driver's seat. It can't be that hard to take it from there. Ya know? The rest of us are totally fucked up, man. You're the onliest one sober."

"Mother of Christ!" Jimmy shouted. "Intartaglia is going to drive! Too cool!"

It's not surprising they won't dare leave the parking lot. Brilliant! I'm thinking, no wonder Eddie was excited.

I'm getting excited trying to get what's going on in my notes, when among the sundry impediments to my understanding already present, like new plot twists and whatever I had recently ingested, were nothing compared to the jolt I got when I saw Mrs. Costa come through Mulcahy's door at 10:33 p.m. to find thirty-odd people engulfed in smoke gaping at them, with her son both on the screen and in the wheelchair she was pushing.

Mrs. Costa left him with Vinnie, who wheeled him through

the crowd cheering: "Eddie. Eddie. Eddie." Eddie said, "Hi." He didn't look happy.

She went outside with Jimmy while I hung by the door to record what was going on both directions, inside on the screen and outside between Barbaro and Mrs. Costa.

Those who were able rushed them before they could get two feet.

"You'll see he gets home, won't ya, Jimmy?"

"Of course, Mrs. Costa. Didn't we always? 'Cept that once." He gathered her bony hands. It was a perfect night for a near-invisible March snow flurry that could only be seen under streetlamps and in front of headlights along the avenues.

"He got dumped in a cab. I don't know how he got up the stairs. He asked to come here." They looked over to the open door as cigarette smoke eked out with cheers from the bar.

"There's a party after somewheres for the cast. Maybe he didn't want to go." Jimmy looked like he wished he was inside with his pals and the show.

"I guess he just didn't fit them or their plans. He said he didn't think they liked him," she said. "What do they expect? Nor that little, lame girl, what's her name? The one with the crutches?"

"Lil'. Lil' Sistah."

"I guess there's better crips around, huh? Had a nice voice, too. I know it's hard to keep clean hoppin' around the streets and up and down the subway stairs."

Mrs. Costa and Jimmy stood for a while. The snow flurry was pleasant.

"Wouldn't he been happier wearing his show clothes on his stool in the parlor, looking at himself doin' his routines in the mirror and his comedy thing twice a year at that place?" Jimmy kept looking at Mulcahy's open door as if he was thinking of sneaking back in.

"All's he's got left is you boys. And me. And I ain't no good. Better than those two floozies and them TV phonies. What's he going to do, Jimmy?"

"I don't know, Mrs. Costa. I'm sorry."

She wouldn't let him walk her home. Nor did Eddie ever tell anyone the whole truth how he and Lil' got fired.

Back inside, the Moons' videotaped episode was almost over. I'd need to interview a bunch of intoxicated eejits to piece anything together. Videotaping was not common practice.

A couple of guys lifted Eddie in his wheelchair onto the bar top near the Philco. Mr. Mulcahy and Augie could hardly rest —stuffing the cash register with money and mopping up the toilet—to complain.

What was happening on screen and in life was hard to allege. Perhaps my notes signified more than they disclosed, because I was often between points of view, unsure if programmed action was actual or imagined, as both were possible.

I was doing my best to cobble things, knowing full well what was on the television at this minute was probably being lost to the ever-receding past.

Then something unexpected happened. Without commotion, Lil' Sistah thumped lightly into the barroom after taking the RR train from Downtown Manhattan to Eighty-Sixth Street, Brooklyn, lowering herself down and up wet and filthy metal and concrete steps with her crutches across her chest, and dragging herself in the lovely snow to Mulcahy's Bar and Grill.

It was the only thing she could think to do, she told me.

When I saw her looking up at the screen, I grabbed Vinnie and we hoisted her onto the bar next to Eddie in his wheelchair, who continued staring at the screen. Meanwhile, the rest of the Moons' routine was unfolding like pouring ingredients into a mixing bowl.

TAKE 1 Ford Fairlane.

ASSEMBLE & MIX:
1 part Eugene driving blind
@ car steering wheel
1 part Eddie in senseless motion
behind driver's seat
1 part Ralph with leash handle tangled
noose-like on hand brake
2 parts Roz pivoting between Eugene
and Sarah to translate and receive signs
2 parts Sarah checking half-remembered streets,
signing directions to Roz for the driver
1 part Lil' Sistah asleep in back
embracing her crutches.

DIRECTIONS:

1 Sprinkle with screams, laughs, street traffic, screeching
brakes, police sirens.

2 Stir in wrong turns, abrupt halts, crashes, mistaken instru-
mentations, and signals.

3 Garnish with arrests, panty shots, attempts to change seats,
and 24th Precinct cells.

4 Fold in hand-held camera, sound equipment, unintended
consequences.

5 Boil until done. Garnish and serve.

Tapes of police vans, armored cars, aircraft, and storm troopers arrive on the scene via taped footage, intersecting images of startled Moons of Saturn faces faded to commercial for colorless, odorless roll-on deodorant in bottle, easy to apply.

Time elapsed: 14.5 minutes.

The Moons' pre-recorded live video had played countrywide in select markets. Inside the bar, people cheered and jumped or dispersed from the TV area to order more beer, go outside for a smoke, walk or drive home.

Dolan, his sister Mary Ellen, Di Paolo, and I joined Lil' and Eddie on the bar top.

The toilet continued sending swill down Ninety-Second Street. Standing on the bar with us was Mickey Lafferty's younger brother Brian, newly arrived after "a heavy date" which wasn't so ponderous. He passed around trembling shots of Johnny Jameson's.

"To everlasting life!" he said.

I made a note of it.

"How did it go?" he asked.

"Great. Except the Moons or the Lampoon or both fired Lil' and Eddie after they taped the show. So—not so much. I suppose they're not the best lookers in the crowd. If you're looking for looks."

Mr. Mulcahy shut the TV off.

Special Eddie and Lil' Sistah sat witness to the blank screen until we remembered to take them down. Lil' said she'd get him home, which I knew she would if she said.

He held her crutches between his legs and over his left shoulder like elephant guns. She leaned on the wheelchair's handles with her elbows and forearms for leverage and off they went toward Fifth Avenue and down Ninety-Second Street, one of the steep Ice Age moraine hills—a fact unknown to anyone there except me.

She leaned into the wheelchair to push them through the streets and over the sidewalks and curbs as the snowflakes dissolved as they landed. I walked behind them on my way home just in case she needed help. Never mind. I should have helped anyway.

"It's easier like this," she said when she saw me. "We're a friggin' human dogsled, Mister! So beat it!"

Mrs. Costa was waiting at the apartment building's front door. She wouldn't let "Sister" go home alone.

"Not in a storm. I'll put Eddie on the sofa. You can stay in his room."

"Nah, Mrs. Costa. I haft'a get home to work in the morning. I've been away so long. Thanks though."

Special Eddie hadn't spoken since he entered the bar. He had to work the words out.

"I'll sleep on the sofa."

Then he said a word I had never heard him say before or since, and that she'd never heard in her whole life in reference to herself.

"Pel-ease."

In the morning, Mrs. Costa found them fluke to prong like grappling hooks on the sofa. She put tea on. Through the window, there was no trace of snow, the sun was pouring in and sidewalks dry. The kettle's hiss called Lil' into the kitchen.

Eddie went into his room to go back to sleep. The women talked things over. How love and pain twined. How Mrs. C. knew Lil' was lying when she told her Eddie said nice things about his mother. They talked about how hard it was to keep clothes "nice." How Lil' would like to wear jewelry, look more like a woman than a plow horse. They spoke of being alone.

Lil' Sistah never went back to the group home and soon gave up her piecework job in Manhattan. Mrs. Costa was glad she had her around to talk to. For the next twenty years, she was one of only two African Americans on the block. Before her, there were none.

Only bedrock endures for long. Man-made things—

macadam streets, buildings, homes, even the bars and convenience stores—get rezoned, repurposed, and built over. Our memories are memories of memories. Without Eddie and Lil', the Moons of Jupiter lasted six months. Mulcahy's didn't make it out of the 1980s, razed to make room for a club with aluminum chairs and a disco lamp. Mrs. Costa left the earth when she felt she could.

Eddie's tag-along life with his diminishing gang of friends shrunk over time due to marriage, the war, and inter-neighborhood migration until his untimely death of wear and tear at fifty-nine in 2008. Lil's lonely life in Brooklyn lasted too long.

In the meantime, while they were together in their way, Lil' taught Eddie a hum-whistle of the Judy Garland Songbook and the complete Motown Sound on their rolling-chair walks around the neighborhood.

After Mrs. Costa's death, Lil' took care of him as much as she could, pushing him every day to the deli where they worked. When it was full-time "Disability" for both, Lil' rigged wheelchairs-for-two with a braided rope side-to-side she'd push with something extra from her strong arms up hills in tandem.

Eddie's power was gone, but he read to her every night whatever he was reading, even if it slowed him down to half his usual rate. Eddie trended toward the classics since high school:

The Bible, Cervantes, Dante, Homer, then on to Dickens, Joyce, T.S. Eliot through E.E. Cummings and the Beats.

For as long as it lasted, Lil' Sistah fell asleep to amazing dreams.

I didn't see everything, but I saw this. Before confronting the hill up Ninety-Second Street for the last time, Eddie and Lil' stretched out across their wheelchairs under a streetlight. Their lips touched, barely perhaps, or symbolically not at all, like an "as if" kiss between the bars of jail cells or through wire cages in the twilight. There on the street where Eddie grew up and Lil' Sistah spent her last days.*

* See Dunne, John. The Life and Times of Edward "Special Eddie" Costa. Lugh of the Sun Press. Self-published, 2010.

The Precambrian Hills
and Rocky Shores of Brooklyn

"I once started out to walk around the
world but ended up in Brooklyn."

—Lawrence Ferlinghetti

Coney Island & Vicinity
Brooklyn, NY
[1954 — 1974]

If you were born and lived in a limestone cave, would you be
more like you or more like me? Or say you spent your life in a
prairie grassland around a lonely pioneer farmhouse, or you're
from a tree-lined New England town. You think you'd be me—
or you?

There was no way people could live like we did on bound-
less plates of rocks, ridges, and outcroppings, with the Hudson
speeding past the bluffs of Bay Ridge and into the vast Atlantic
without it having an effect.

Whether we knew it or not, which we didn't, the evidence
was everywhere. Sea fog engulfed us in the mornings and
evenings, and gulls yelled at us all day. Highways dead-ended
into polluted inlets and river views or turned into ocean
beaches fronted by collapsing boardwalks and discarded
machinery.

Our apartments and flats soared over and dipped into
Precambrian hills and valleys that were paved over for
hundreds of years by macadam, asphalt, and concrete. It was
hard to visualize or think about, and we didn't, even though 450
million years prior, Pangaea propelled the land around here
miles into the sky.

Some things can't be said and may be inconceivable.

One day, I think, when I was nine, a 60-ton, 75-foot-long

finback whale washed up onto the beach off the Brooklyn resort town of Coney Island—a once-in-a-lifetime visit from the depths of the limitless ocean. In a few days, the smell would make you want to puke.

"Come on, Mickie," my dad whispered to evade my younger brother and sister after breakfast one Saturday, grabbing his coat and fedora.

"Wanna see the whale?"

They would make a production out of it, which I could tell he wasn't up for. Not today. Too large a death for the very young. My stepmother was going nowhere. Besides, I soon found he wanted—maybe needed—an evocative walk along the seedy corners and dives of Surf and Stillwell Avenues; things he lost from memory from his youth in the '20s and '30s, but were now shimmering ghosts in his chest. Even if they were garish and cheap.

It'd hard to talk about fleeting things. Why he needed me along was a mystery. Perhaps he thought I was him.

The whale had been dragged from a nearby beach to an alley behind Nathan's Famous Hot Dogs. The price of dead-whale viewing had just been cut in half to 25 cents because of the stench.

I think what my dad wanted was to get his last chance to see the freak shows, gather dying glimpses of his youth in the shrinking crowds that used to be huge, when over a million people would be delivered to Surf Avenue and the Boardwalk on summer weekends by the newly constructed Stillwell Avenue Subway.

The same itch that gets people to stare at an accident victim dying in the road or touch the face of a beloved relative in the coffin. Who knows? I didn't need to be asked twice.

. . .

Freak shows were freak shows and dead whales were dead whales, and everything and everywhere was going out of style.

Between the fossilized dreams and smell of the greasepaint, Old Brooklyn was dying, as it was always, to be replaced, revamped, renewed, and cycled away by what was coming next, whatever that was. For Coney Island, it was high-rise housing projects and chain stores.

My father heard about the whale at the pool room. The two local papers gave it scant coverage, like it was a sad memento of God's initial creation, which it was not. Fifty million years before we arrived today, whales could walk, I found out years later. Like dogs or pigs. What did we know? The rotting whale didn't know either. For some reason, I connected with it. I don't know why.

I think my dad did, too. We didn't talk about it. What could we say? We drove down Ocean Parkway, a direct route through the middle of Brooklyn to the ocean and Coney Island, affording close-up views of neighborhoods where mostly women and small children engaged in early summer sunbathing on aluminum folding chairs.

My dad liked watching families walking home from synagogue with children skipping semi-circles along the sidewalks in their somber Sabbath clothing or checking the kids out playing stickball or Double Dutch, if the timing was right. It was all guesswork.

When we arrived at Coney Island, we drove past Nathan's, the bars, the cheap circus-like attractions, and the tunnel of love along Surf Avenue until we found a place to park.

Walking back toward the action, we said nothing. It wasn't so much we didn't speak as there was nothing to say, and it was a new world for me of sights, smells, and sounds unfolding like dirty laundry as cheesy attractions on both sides of the avenue became frequent, some with barkers barking about the delights and potential dangers inside.

Eerie, fake laughter and diabolical calliope melodies leaked from behind the doors and entrances in sympathy. As the filth and garbage gathered more and more by the curb, a verb-to-be-ness came over my dad.

The 700 Pound Lady. Lionel the Lion-Faced Man. Lobster Boy. The Tattooed Lady. Luna Park and The Dime Museum. My father didn't seem to care for these things per se, but remembered feeling them the way he did as a boy and young man. The bars, the Cyclone, the Wild Mouse, the Parachute Ride along the Boardwalk, a Midget City of 300 midgets like out of The Wizard of Oz. Then more freaks along Surf Avenue where 5-ton elephants slid down chutes into a pool.

It wasn't so much the stuff of his life he was looking for as it was looking for himself—the way he used to feel in everything and everything all together. Eddie's Souvenirs. Turtle Girl and Carl, the Alligator Man. Sodom by the Sea. The possibilities appalling!

Sometimes he'd compare today's sights and happenings with the way things were. "The people, everything seemed bigger then."

I was thinking maybe he was smaller.

"I guess maybe I was smaller," he said. My dad and I were like that sometimes.

The Carousel Pigs and the WHIP rides were next and The Dancing Lovelies "As You Like It." The man you stuck pins in for a quarter and the woman with two arms and four legs. Willie's Pizzerio. The Conjoined Twins.

The Surf Hotel and the Half-Moon where my mom and him honeymooned for a night before he was inducted.

The whale was yards away. There was a tent. It was lit by bare lightbulbs hung from electric wires.

Newly hatched blowflies buzzed, spreading God's filth. But it was the cooking of the embalming fluid and rotting flesh that was unbearable. We stood staring at the head. Its jaws were shut and eyes closed and its lips were horribly wrinkled and folded into its lower jaw. Monster lips stretched yellow and olive green or were painted. Its back and sides were a sleek, brownish-black, with a contrasting white underbelly. Was it the whale my father came to see? Or the freaks and the sights and sounds of the amusements?

I thought about these things for many years growing up. It wasn't troubling; it was just mysterious. We certainly didn't talk about it. We stood in front of the whale for a long time.

We drove home, mostly in silence. It was the best lesson I ever got, although I'd be damned if I knew what to say it was. Something to do with how to be. About how not everything comes with words.

Mulcahy's Bar & Grill
92nd Street and 5th

Twenty years later, I got, "Hey Mick. Why's Third Avenue such a hump to walk up to, like it's Mount Freakin' Olympus or something?"

We were in Mulcahy's Bar & Grill. My dad was barely alive up the block in Victory Memorial Hospital. My stepmom was with him. He wasn't doing so great. I would relieve her in an hour.

"I don't know, Richie. I hear there's a dump of bedrock like a mile deep underneath the pavement, like from a gigantic glacier. Makes no sense. Who knows? This one's on me."

"'Bout time."

"I know."

What happened next was lost to the receding past and proceeding future. It's just as well.

Along the high-rise and rowhouse ledges, common Brooklyn rock pigeons with iridescent purple heads dozed, shadows of rooftops inched to the opposite sides of the streets, and a gray squirrel rattled its tail at a telephone wire hanging from a pole.

Cars and trucks tracked into and out of bridge entrances and exits into the city and out onto the continent. A squadron of blackbirds played looping chords in patterns sensitive to barometric disquiets, the click of the bird brain to dive and soar, and other offices of fate like a drop of black ink plunged into a glass of water in the sky.

Parents who never graduated elementary school help kids get their masters.

Mail was removed from a mailbox by a mailman, and three

street dogs turned the corner fixing for a fight. Road crews razed every drib of concrete and asphalt with jackhammers. Babies were born.

Mansions and slums were repurposed. Mrs. Mary Daily News and Pool Room Jack eat breakfast with Dostoyevsky–Shakespeare teens. Buildings rose on the metamorphic schist up the hill near Fourth Avenue. While it rose, two were demolished to make room for fresh families; a funeral procession left McLaughlin's for Queens.

Politicians and gangsters found new ways to get rich. Democrats and Republicans replaced each other, parents picked up children, encountered others, twenty tankers crisscrossed with cargoes. The Hudson's tide swelled, lowered, lowered and swelled every moment, and everything kept going and coming, always, and what can anyone do or say about any of it?

Gerry Coleman
Brooklyn [1947]

ABOUT THE AUTHOR

Award-winning storyteller Gerry Coleman brings four decades of literary expertise and a passion for the human experience to every page he writes.

His compelling short fiction has earned recognition across multiple publications, including a Best Story award in the Short Fiction Category at the prestigious "Writers In Paradise" Conference.

Readers can find his work in *The Pavan*, *The Saratoga Scene Magazine*, *Literally Stories*, and *Stories from Around The World*, where his authentic voice and keen insight into human nature captivates audiences year after year.

Drawing from his rich Brooklyn roots and extensive academic background—including doctoral work in Educational Psychology at Columbia University—he brings a unique combination of street-smart authenticity and scholarly depth that infuses his storytelling with both heart and intelligence.

Now based in Florida, Gerry continues his mission to elevate the craft of writing. He organizes dynamic writer salons and workshops for WordSmittenWorkShop, helps coordinate events for The Authors Guild's Tampa Bay Chapter, and provides personalized consulting for writers developing full-length book projects. His mentorship has helped countless authors find their voice and bring their stories to life.

His stories don't just entertain—they linger long after the last page is turned.

Thank You for Reading

Ninety-Second Street, Brooklyn Stories
by Gerry Coleman

If you enjoyed reading this book, please consider leaving a review on your preferred platform. Your feedback supports quality content and helps inspire future releases.

Want more from the Brooklyn Writers Press?

Browse our complete catalog.
brooklynwriterspress.com